OP 1st 7⁵ᶜ

FABLES

FABLES

by Jacquetta Hawkes

London

The Cresset Press

1953

First published in 1953 *by*

The Cresset Press

11 *Fitzroy Square, London, W*1

and printed in Great Britain by

The Shenval Press, London and Hertford

TO
NICOLAS HAWKES

Contents

THE FABLES

The Nature of a Red Admiral

L IFE IN THE walled Garden was very well ordered. On
one side of the broad path traversing it, vegetables
and fruit trees grew, on the other flowers and
flowering shrubs.

The vegetables owed much of their attractiveness to
symmetry. The silvery plants of cabbage and cauliflower
were as regularly spaced as guardsmen; passing insects
and birds were delighted by the diagonal vistas that
flickered through their ranks. Carrots made fluffy green
hedges, beetroot glossy purple ones; embanked lines of
potato and leek showed as neat corrugations, while taller
than all and more brightly coloured were the green and
red tents of the runner beans.

To this visible landscape was added the realm of smells
extending round the herb bed. The aromatic thyme had
victory alike over the freshness of mint, the vulgar jolly
stink of chive and the heavy rancour of sage; behind them
the rue was tall and bitter.

The whole vegetable side of the Garden expressed seriousness of purpose, an earnest pregnancy. At all seasons, but most noticeably in summer, the walls contained this atmosphere of physical activity; roots orange, white, brown and purple were swelling underground; seeds of marbled pink and black were waxing inside their closely fitting pods; tiny fruits prepared to grow plump and rosy. All must be fertile, must increase to fill their appointed place in the Garden.

The flowers had neither the mathematical precision nor the indwelling sense of purpose found among the vegetables. They were content merely to be, to exist in the pride of their colours, shapes and scents, of their delicacy or magnificence. They had only to put forth the blossoms expressing their praise of life to find fulfilment.

Along their own side of the central path the flowers made a richly variegated ramp, sloping up from the double daisies at the verge, buttons of dense crimson fur, to the sweet pink masses, the slender spires, of stocks and delphiniums. Beyond this border each species had its own territory, its regiment, where each could prove its distinctive quality. At one extreme there was the sombre foliage of chrysanthemums waiting until all their rivals were spent to burn in yellow, chestnut and bronze; at the other the immediate gaiety of sweet peas, pretty nitwits flowering upon their screens as though they had just alighted, a cloud of butterflies with pink, white and lilac wings.

There were vast numbers of insects living in the Garden. Some of them did the plants service, fertilizing them, killing their pests, pleasuring them with their light

2

feet, while others were hostile, burrowing into buds and destroying their promise, munching away at their roots, cutting discs from their leaves and injecting them with poisons that crippled their growth or blemished their beauty. Yet whether the insects appeared to work on the plants for good or ill they depended upon one another, living together, as any community must, in a web of dependency intricate and easily destroyed as a spider's.

Nothing within the Garden was more important to its inhabitants than the containing walls. The soft, rose-coloured bricks, which had been there beyond all memory and had evidently been created by the powers of the Outside, were full of crannies where insects could be snugly housed and where floating seeds could lodge, thrust down hair-fine roots and put forth the particular stem, leaves and flower already determined in the floating seed. As for the peaches and pears on the southward-facing wall, they were the aristocrats of the garden; the severe discipline of their training, the stiff formality of their limbs, being rewarded by the luscious perfection of the fruit they bore. But it was the four walls themselves that gave the Garden its significance, all that inspired it with consciousness and pride of being. What can be more important than an outline, than the skin which separates an entity from the rest of being? No one fully understood the world beyond the walls; it was only known there were huge trees, wide expanses of grass, strange monsters of many kinds and the House.

All the inhabitants of the Garden were aware of Outside forces beyond their comprehension. The arrival and disappearance of plants, fruits and seed, the cutting off of flowers in their prime, were more obviously mysterious even than the rise and fall of seasons. They were enough to convince the plants, both flowers and vegetables, that there were supernatural powers demanding a religious awe. The insects had rather less experience of supernatural phenomena, but the occasional holocausts which decimated whole settlements encouraged them to superstition and magical practices, if not to religious faith.

This is the moment at which to introduce the creature which was certainly the most important as well as the most beautiful denizen of the Garden. A Red Admiral butterfly, a splendid presence with its dark, velvety wings emblazoned with holy symbols in scarlet and white. The Garden insects felt exalted by their relationship with this far more noble and ethereal being; the vegetables found he gave them confidence in the value of their work, while the flowers knew that their own loveliness, their own striving after perfection, were caught up and magnified through the existence of the Red Admiral. Every plant felt its colours more brilliant, its scent sweeter and its whole form idealized on those days when the butterfly alighted upon it and poised, caressing its petals with delicately barbed feet, while alternately spreading its wings to the sun, or closing them tip to tip as though in prayer.

The entire population shared the belief that the Red Admiral existed as an intermediary between themselves and the mysterious Outside powers of the House. When, as occasionally happened, it gave a few tremendous beats of its wings, rose, and floated over the wall, absenting itself

4

for a while, they were confident that their messenger was among the powers, possibly in the house itself, and that it would return laden with divinity like a bee with honey.

For long, no one knew how long, the life of the Garden had gone its round without change. Then gradually, and at first inconspicuously, a change began. It was initiated by the insects. Some of the sharper witted and more predatory species infected the inhabitants of the Garden with the idea that they were living in a shameful state of ignorance and backwardness. The leaders of this movement were the solitary wasps who had their nests in the crannies of the wall, and the ichneumon-flies who spent much of their time hanging round the cabbages waiting to stab and impregnate the helpless green caterpillars feeding there.

The clever insects preached enlightenment. You look at one another, they said, and you call this plant a daisy, that insect a ladybird, but have these terms any real meaning? Surely we should all look closer and more objectively, try to discover the nature of the reality behind these traditional names. 'Ladybird' indeed! The term evidently embodies some historical tradition, but our researches have already convinced us that the organism concerned is neither a lady nor a bird, and such anachronisms are not good enough for a progressive people. How can we go on living, buzzed the wasps as they darted irritably from void to void, without understanding how anything functions, what are the laws controlling our being, or what, indeed, we *really* are? We must experiment, we must use mental discipline in the practice of objective analysis until we can find the true answers.

Their first experiments were ingenious and harmless. The wasps obliged their humble cousins the hover-flies to hover for hours on end above the purple carpet of the thyme. They then carefully scraped their wings, examined the deposits through all the facets of their eyes and announced that the seemingly delicious scent of the herb was in fact no more than minute volatile particles of an oleaginous substance. A green caterpillar, which had died very slowly after the loathsome eruption from its side of the ichneumon larvae, was proved to consist simply of a cellular plasma contained within a transparent sac, furnished with instruments of propulsion and mastication and with an inherent potentiality to evolve into a wing-bearing insect.

The other insects, who found both the language and modes of thought quite novel, were naturally very much impressed. They recognized it as a proof of the amazing penetration of their kind that they were now able to state all these facts about the true nature of what before had seemed utterly mysterious. The flowers and other plants were much less inclined to feel admiration for the investigators; perhaps they were too stupid fully to understand the importance of the discoveries made by the wasps and ichneumons. The flowers went on spreading their petals, the vegetables plumping themselves, all of them keeping a dim, hazy faith in the larger patterns of which blossoming and fruition were a part. No doubt the insects were brilliantly clever, but, after all, life remained.

Once the insects had realized the analytical strength of their brains, they could not restrain their activity. These brains had become as sharp and pitiless as their own stings and ovipositors. Inevitably in time they were attracted towards the religious sentiments of the Garden which were so influential though impalpable a part of its existence. Just because they were impalpable it was absolutely necessary to find some material manifestation upon which their analytical weapons could be turned with effect. The Red Admiral was the most wonderful, supposedly the holiest creature known; would it not benefit everyone to learn more facts about the butterfly so that they might have a deeper understanding of its nature, this bearer of intimations of divinity? Knowledge was now accepted as a glorious prerogative of the people of the Garden; to honour the Red Admiral in ignorance would be to dishonour their own highest faculties.

All the plants and many of the insects were against this idea, indeed some of them were deeply shocked, an emotion which provoked even greater energy among the supporters by enabling them to denounce such obscurantism, such denial of the light. Indeed, opposition of this kind magnified the self-esteem of the analysts; not for them emotional cowardice and superstition, they flew in the cold light of reason, with the courage to face facts however bitter they might be.

The opposition might have been more effective had anyone believed it to be possible to take or to analyse the Red Admiral; most people vaguely assumed this to be the sort of plan which could be supported or resisted in theory, but never carried out. There are forces as well as meanings beyond comprehension, a truth which the insects exploited even while they denied it. The wasps and their assistants, the hover-flies, made cunning plans to entice and trap the Red Admiral, yet although the butterfly could easily have eluded all their trickery, in practice it never had to be tried. The urge of their intellectual curiosity had become irresistible, it was now a living part of the Garden, and the noble victim submitted to it as though he were caught in a net woven of pure will. He settled on a ledge of the wall, opened his once vaunting wings and remained passive while a host of his inferiors began their tests. It was a strange and tragic sight to see a creature, possessed of beauty and imagination so far beyond theirs, submitting to the curiosity of a swarm of ugly insects.

The very first examination convinced the wasps that the supposed holy symbols on the Red Admiral's wings were an appearance only, for in fact they were composed of many thousand tiny plates overlapping one another like the scales of a snake. The weevils, now pressed into service for the sake of their exceptional dexterity, were ordered to detach these plates and count the numbers of each colour.

The weevils went to and fro mutilating the butterfly which they had for so long revered. They were executing orders. The plates were ranged in rows on several large, shiny pear leaves, and at last the weevils were able to report that the upper surface of the wings consisted of one hundred thousand black plates, fifty thousand red and twenty thousand white. The underside of the same wings was so subtly variegated that not even a rough estimate was possible.

Meanwhile the wasps themselves had taken many specimens of the silky black hairs adorning the butterfly's body, magnified them with a dewdrop, and found them to be mere trichoid growths of circular section and melanistic pigmentation.

The inquisitiveness, the analytical urge of the investigators grew with exercise until they became a lust as irresistible as that which drove the males to mount on to the brittle backs of the females. Unable to check their compulsive desire to know, they committed outrages against their former idol. One of the leading wasps used his sharp jaws to amputate the left hand of the two antennae, those exquisitely sensitive organs which many of the plants had believed to be tuned to receive intimations from Outside. Another wasp in examining the articulation of the joint broke off a leg at the knee, while the most ruthless of the ichneumon punctured the delicate abdomen with his ovipositor, drawing off a fluid which was identified by the name of abdodivernalfluovine.

With each of these atrocious acts the whole body of the Red Admiral was convulsed and his wings trembled, yet he made no effort to escape; he might have been impaled upon the wall.

Their powers of analysis exhausted, the investigators flew round the Garden proclaiming that the Red Admiral had now been explained. He consisted of an abdominal sac filled with abdodivernalfluovine and bearing melanistic trichoid growths; the head carried two capillary appendices with neural passages. As for the wings, which had appeared to be so significant, they were nothing but transparent membranes overlain with one hundred thousand melanistic units of pigmentation, fifty thousand rufoid and twenty thousand albinoid units. These were the true facts, and it was greatly to the glory of the Garden that this truth was now established, the dark cloud of superstition and ignorance rolled back a little further.

After this announcement had been made throughout the Garden nearly all the flowers rustled together murmuring, 'Yes, Oh yes?' in their vague way; but a clump of peonies, whose sleek round buds had just burst into crimson bloom, shouted out 'Nonsense! And where is the Red Admiral, our messenger? His is the glory we can understand and share.'

'Yes. Where, where?' the flowers repeated, turning their eyes hither and thither.

'There he is,' said the foremost solitary wasp a little defiantly, 'there on the ledge of the wall. Naturally it was impossible to restore the organism after analysis. We must be prepared to make sacrifices in the cause of truth.'

The inhabitants of the Garden, who all this time had hardly appreciated what was going on among them, and who had been so ready to listen to the fashionable talk of the analysts, now looked in alarm towards the wall. At first they saw nothing, but then a ghostly figure moved on the ledge; as slowly as a snail and far more unsteadily it lurched forward, tipping over on its side at every step.

Reaching the edge, this apparition paused for a respite, quivering, before it launched into the air where it could scarcely maintain itself.

Murmurs, protests and shrieks came from the flowers, the vegetables groaned or cursed and the insects broke into a sibilant wail of dismay. Pitifully struggling to keep itself afloat was a spectral creature, the wings reduced to buckled membranes, transparent and quite colourless save for a few poor smudges still clinging to the underside. Gone were the splendid black velvety wings charged with their symbols in scarlet and white. This barely visible ghost was more remote from the living butterfly than is a skeleton leaf from the sappy foliage of spring.

For a moment longer it wavered in the air, then a current of air seemed to lift it over the wall and out of sight. Perhaps a passing bird thought it just worth while to snap it up, but its fate is of no significance, for this thing was no longer the Red Admiral butterfly. He had been destroyed and would never be seen again in the Garden.

The City of the Cats

THE CITY OF the Cats was beautiful. Even the Dogs were aware of its fantastic beauty. It stood near the head of a valley at the point where a grey cataract of rocks was giving way to a level bottom striped with meadows. In these fertile meadows grazed the herds of creamy white cattle which provided the citizens with all the food they needed. A little higher up the valley, mountain streams rushing down between the rocks, sometimes in a tense, plaited silence of dark water, sometimes breaking into noisy white falls, united in a single river, to flow swift but untroubled through the city and the fields below it.

The Cats' houses can best be likened to pagodas, for they were lighter and more intricate than any Gothic spire. It was the custom for each new generation, when it inherited the family dwelling, to carve and paint another tier to be added to the summit of the spire—a practice which had resulted in a curious diversity. Yet the diversity was always harmonious; the slender houses rose from

their slopes with the grace and perfect grouping of chestnut blossom on a spreading branch. In their gardens, all
of which were private, the Cats grew rare varieties of
everlasting-flower, aloes, and the cactuses whose brilliant
petals break so unexpectedly from the harsh body of the
plant.

The city was enclosed by walls which showed pleasing
irregularities of height and direction as they followed the
contours of the ground. Because it had become unusual
for any Cat to go beyond the walls, many of the gates had
fallen into disuse, some being converted into fountains,
others into niches for the reception of statues. Only a small
wicket on the upper side of the town and a large gate-
house on the lower remained open. The rampart walks,
too, once vigilantly patrolled by the city guard, had lapsed
wholly into peacefulness. They now offered a delightful
promenade where the younger citizens could take the air
after dark.

During certain periods of the day, and most universally
during the hour before sunset, the Cats would retire into
their houses, seat themselves with their tails curled tightly round their paws, and then, by feline concentration,
whip themselves into more and more exalted realms of
meditation. They sat absolutely motionless, even the tips
of their tails poised and still. Only the black pupils of their
eyes dilated and contracted again within the tawny circle
of the iris.

For many generations now, the purr of these Cats had
ceased to make any sound audible to the normal ear,
but, as they sat in contemplation, their bodies vibrated

13

with an unseen intensity which caused tremors to run through the delicate fabric of the houses and sound the swarms of little bells hanging on hair-fine threads in every tier of the pagodas. So it was that during the contemplative hours a harmony of exquisite felicity hung like a cloud about the city. Joining with the natural music of the waterfalls it would float up the valley.

It was down the valley that the Dogs had their residential suburb: many rows of comfortable kennels, all with identical gabled roofs and all painted either bottle-green or plum. The life work of the Dogs was to tend the Cats. They looked after their cattle, scavenged their streets and kept their houses clean and in order. The better bred of the young bitches were employed as personal maids to groom the Cats' silken coats and to wash and anoint their idle-tender paws. All these tasks had been done by the Dogs from time beyond memory; they did them submissively enough while in the sight of their masters, but round the kennels there was often the growling and whining of discontent.

Among the Cats, the proportion of kittens was becoming smaller and smaller. Litters of more than two were never born (or if they were, because such grossness would have provoked social ostracism, the totals were discreetly adjusted). Newborn kittens were given small bitches as wet-nurses, and were afterwards segregated in boarding-schools. These schools were staffed by Cats whose faulty powers of vibration barred them from society; either they suffered the embarrassment of an audible purr or their vibrations were too weak, too little concentrated, to produce a true bell harmony. The teachers were so much aware of these shortcomings, however, that no other Cats could have imposed a more exact discipline in training the kittens to develop the powers and accomplishments which they themselves lacked.

Besides these schools the only other public establishment occupied a large house on the outskirts of the city. All the citizens knew of its existence, but they were far too well-bred to make it a subject for conversation; when, occasionally, it had to be mentioned it was spoken of simply as the Establishment. Here numbers of mice were kept, and young Cats of both sexes. It was an exceedingly well-conducted institution and outwardly decorous.

Although the Cats always ignored the fact, neither they nor their Dog servants could fail to notice how surely the population of the city was declining; dozens of houses stood empty and their spires silent. As a result some of the Dogs were out of work and hung about thinking savagely of the big litters squirming in the corners of the kennels at home. To a sensitive visitor it would have been clear that some long-maintained balance, some delicate adjustment of stresses, was about to be upset.

The hour found its inevitable instrument. A clever mongrel who had forfeited his job as confidential servant to the Chief Conductor of the city, worked skilfully upon the general discontent. He exhorted his fellows to take courage and end their servitude to useless, vicious and exacting masters. One evening when the bell music was at its height and the valley full of the ravishing sound, a fearful clamour broke out in the Dogs' suburb, a hideous medley of barks of every pitch. Behind their leader, the Dogs crowded up the valley to attack the city. Perfect order had existed for so long that the Cats had neglected to appoint a single watchman or sentinel. The gates were opened by a master from the Tom-kittens' school, embittered into treachery by a conviction that his purr had been falsely pronounced to be audible.

It was a matter of quick butchery. The Cats, high in their ecstatic contemplation, could not descend to notice a physical danger, and it is doubtful had they done so whether they would have seen fit either to fly or to resist. As it was, the bells of every inhabited pagoda sounded until the very last moment. When the slaughter was over (and in the confusion even the treacherous schoolmaster was not spared) the larger Dogs set to work to destroy all the houses, whose fine appointments they could not enjoy. Soon the river was full of carved spars and painted panels jostling down towards the sea. The thousands of bells, breaking from their hair suspension, sank down and gathered for a moment in lovely shoals along the river bottom. They drifted there as transparent as noon-day moons, grew yet fainter until they resembled the hardly lit burden of a new moon, then disappeared. Silenced already by the water, now they were for ever choked in mud.

The next few days the Dogs spent in dragging up their kennels to the site of the destroyed city—the mongrel taking good care that his went to the place where formerly the Chief Conductor's pagoda had stood. When the work was finished and the Dog's suburb looked almost exactly the same in its new position as it had done before the move, a tremendous feast was held. Scores of the Cats' milch cows were eaten flesh and bone together, washed down with fermented milk found in the cellars of the Establishment. Afterwards there was a mighty outburst of baying to the moon.

Once the feast was over, the Dogs could find no further source of jubilation. The food was much as before, the kennels were not greatly improved by the tasteless application of Cat paints, and the Dogs could find no change in themselves that was not for the worse. They were suffering from a terrible formlessness and lack of purpose in their new, free lives. A number of the bitches, those who had been lady's-maids or wet-nurses, were frankly heartbroken by the loss of their mistresses or charges, and their emotion soon affected their mates. There was faction and unrest to fill the vacancy of the days; several murders culminated in the disappearance of the mongrel in circumstances which could not be explained until his body was found in the river.

After this a few of the more responsible Dogs formed a Council to debate what should be done. Their meetings were unprofitable because not only were the Councillors quite incapable of understanding what was wrong, but no one of them individually would admit anything was wrong at all. After several Councils had broken up in snappish irritability, a suitable solution was agreed: it consisted of shifting responsibility to a higher authority.

The Dogs knew their former masters had reverenced a mysterious person who lived in a cave beside the small, black mountain lake at the very top of the valley. Ceremonial visits had been regularly paid him by the Cats, for it was he who made the bells on which their music depended. Gathering rock crystal on the mountains he carved it into domes as thin as bubbles, and inside fixed clappers of ground and polished crystals. The clappers hung like bright, petrified tears; the Cats had always believed that the threads which tied them were the Bell-Maker's own hairs. This Bell-Maker possessed a most extraordinary sense of pitch, and there is no doubt that his profession had empowered him to create and control the marvellous harmony of all the city bells in unison.

No Dog had ever before approached his cave, but now a small deputation mounted through the wicket gate and wound up between the rocks. Following a narrow track worn by the Cats, its members were conscious of clumsiness and of the gross size and hairiness of their paws. At last they were led to the cave by a beam of darkness cutting through the sunshine, yet inside they could not detect the source from which it shone; indeed, they could see nothing at all. They called to the Bell-Maker, begging him to show himself and command them what they should do.

No one came, but words seemed to shape themselves in the beam.

'I never appeared in person even to the Cats. I will tell you, as I told them, to imagine me as fulfilling your own ideal conception of yourselves. This saves trouble, for whatever I may say or do, you are certain to make that mistake. What do you want of me?'

'Sire,' they replied, 'we killed the Cats because they were vile parasites upon us Dogs. We thought everything would be much better without them, but it hasn't turned out quite as we expected, and now our lives are both dull and unsafe. We beg you not to blame us for the death of the Cats; we exterminated them because we believed it to be our duty to rid the world of such worthless creatures.'

'Much as I miss the harmony which rose up from the city and brought me the food of rapture, I do not blame you any more than I blame them; the situation was too much for you. I condemn you only for the self-delusion which makes you attempt to disguise your very natural greed and jealousy with talk of duty and high moral purposes. If you will repent this, and also the arrogance you showed in assuming that any change you made in the old order must be for the better, I will do what I can to help you to serve me and yourselves.'

The Dogs all drooped their tails as a mark of their grateful humility, and the Bell-Maker went on:

'First you must impose a severe discipline upon yourselves. Give your life shape by setting limits upon it. You should not eat so much or such coarse food, you should neither bark so loudly and senselessly when you are pleased nor snarl and quarrel at other times. Without weakening them, you must constantly deny and prune your lusts. In such details as your personal habits, you should take scrupulous care of your coats until perhaps you may make them finer and more silky; it would be no bad thing to introduce some artificial fashions such as shaping your ears or docking your tails. You should always be ready to listen to the advice of the bitches and to try to please them, for they will instinctively understand these matters better than you can.

'When you have persevered in such disciplines you may find you are less clumsy and more able to make things of some beauty. You might start by improving the architecture and decoration of your kennels; then, because you are by nature more gregarious than the Cats, you would probably get great satisfaction from noble public buildings. Finally, you must labour to rise to purposes altogether higher. I doubt whether you will ever achieve anything comparable to the harmonies of the Cats, but between us we must try to intensify and shape your instinct for baying at the moon. And don't forget that if you are to do these things really well you will have to find willing servants. Now leave me, and perhaps in a century your descendants may accomplish something.'

The rest of the Dogs shambled down the hill much bewildered by what they had been told, but the most intelligent of them stayed behind to say :

'But Sire, High Bell-Maker, if we do as you have commanded, shall we not grow very much like the Cats whom we have destroyed?'

'No,' the words slid quietly down the beam, 'not like the Cats; that is your absolute justification. If you are both diligent and fortunate you may perhaps learn to express the essence of your kind. Go and see what you can do, but remember, it is likely enough you will fail altogether. The Cats, after all, were a most remarkable people.'

20

The Fountain

ROM THE IONIC portico of the mansion a double
flight of stone steps, heavily balustraded, led past the
terrace to the ornamental garden below. At the foot
of each flight, between the last voluptuous curves of the
balustrade and the first flower beds, stood a white marble
lady. These two ladies, timid Victorian Venuses, were
identical except that one was the mirror image of the
other. They were leaning slightly forward, their shoulders
nervously bent, one had her left foot, the other her right
foot, raised on a neat, fern-enveloped boulder; one
clutched in her left hand, the other in her right hand,
the corner of a cloth, about the size of a tea towel, which
she was drawing across her pubic triangle; their lips were
parted; a straying lock of hair curled over the left and
right shoulders.

Neither lady has anything whatever to do with this
story, except that the direction of their gaze, from eyes
carefully provided with iris and pupil on their glistening
marble surfaces, serves to lead the attention to its goal—

the fountain which played at the centre of the ornamental garden.

This fountain had a spacious stone basin where a dozen elderly goldfish, fluffy with fungus, hung about among the stems of the lily leaves whose disks paved the surface of the water. On a pedestal rising through the leaves a plump, stocky cherub in cast bronze was blowing upon a long horn; hidden from sight, a lead pipe ran up through the cherub's body and the horn, conducting the gush of water which spouted from the mouth of the instrument as a liquid substitute for sound.

The water jet was certainly the best part of the fountain; indeed, it was impossible to suspend disbelief at the sight of so small a boy, his cheeks only gently puffed, blowing aloft a column of water to more than four times his own height. The shining column rose to eight feet before feathering out, losing force and falling. Sometimes in rough weather the drops would stream away with the wind, making a dark oval on the gravel, but normally they fell back into the basin where some of them would lie on the lily leaves, bright as diamonds but rounded like pearls. It was a noble fountain, and one that never failed, or even fluctuated, for it was supplied by a little stream flowing down from the chalk.

On summer nights when visitors at the mansion strayed out on to the terrace and moved like figures in a shadow play before the luminous windows (silhouettes that changed shape with the changing fashions) they could hear the fountain rustling far below them in the darkness. When a full moon was hanging at their backs they might even be able to distinguish its form, slender and ghostly pale, perpetual yet always swiftly moving.

For fifty years the fountain had played and had delighted all who saw or heard it, yet for fifty years the water had muttered angrily against its lot.

'Here am I, a living stream. I could fill a broad channel if I were allowed to flow unconfined, but tyrants forced me into this dark pipe, unto this piece of plumbing. O for liberation! How I crave to express my whole nature, to fulfil myself to the limit of my capacities.'

So the water muttered as it rose and fell; so it complained even when rainbows stood in its spray, or a dozen human beings came to admire its splendours. Yet in the basin it lay silent, heavy with minute vegetable life, darkened by lily leaves and given movement only by the falling drops and the idle passage of fishes.

One summer there was a long, burning drought. Every evening the gardeners came to water the variegated cushions of pink, purple and magenta blossoms which their misguided skill had puffed up in the flower beds. The open park surrounding the garden turned from fresh green to cardboard colour. Soon the grass was not only sere but tumbled and fouled for it was made to receive a large herd of bullocks, let into the park when their own pastures were exhausted. Daily the grass grew poorer, and the dung-bred flies multiplied; the bullocks would stand in the narrow shade of one of the fenced tree-clumps pushing, flicking and twitching until suddenly the limit of their stolid acquiescence was passed and they would all career frantically to another clump of trees.

At the height of a particularly sweltering afternoon when one of the bullocks was stampeding across the park in this fashion he heard the rustle of the fountain; he had heard it often before, its ceaseless complaints of oppression sounding in his ears as promises of refreshment and escape from tormenting flies, but never before had there been any chance of reaching it. This afternoon the gate leading into the ornamental garden had been left open. The bullock was one in whom the parental genes had been fortunately combined, resulting in an animal of more than average enterprise and ability. He broke away from the herd, made for the gate and in a moment was on the smoothly raked gravel, swinging his head and shuffling his hoofs while appraising these strange surroundings. At first he was troubled by the presence of the two Venuses whose limbs were gleaming in the sun like uncut sugar-loaves (even at night, now, the marble of their flesh was never cold), but presently the intelligent beast decided they were incapable of movement and trotted towards the fountain, the flies making a noisy halo behind his head. The bullock lowered his muzzle to the water, where each nostril sent its own system of concentric ripples widening across the surface. He drank, then set his forefeet into the basin; gingerly he muzzled his way forward through the delicious coolness until he was standing beside the cherub, with the smooth snaky stem of a water lily hanging over one horn and the fountain sprinkling his dusty pelt.

A harmless, thankful creature he dawdled there until his peace was disturbed by uncouth shouts, by the rattle of boots on the steps and at last by the appearance of a young gardener running towards him with a brandished hoe. The bullock swung round to escape, his hoofs slipped on the slimy, curving stone bottom, and, as he lurched, several hundredweight of beef and bone struck the cherub's little brazen flank. The metal snapped at the ankle joints and a moment later the leaden pipe also gave way. For an instant a detached column of water stood in the air, then fell, the last flower of the long struggle between stream and pipe. The poor beast recovered its balance, dragged itself from the basin and with a veil of green algae clinging to its coat fled back into the park.

Meanwhile the owner had hurried down to join the gardener in surveying the damaged fountain. The winged boy was submerged, though the tip of his trumpet projected through the water; he was lying propped on his pinions, and the goldfish, emerging from the hiding places they had sought to avoid the bullock's hairy legs, were already exploring the inmost parts of his body. Entering through the ankles, they flicked their passage through the tunnels formed by the legs, then circled belly and head in languid enjoyment.

The cherub's feet, ending in jagged edges, were still clamped to the pedestal; through the left one, where the pipe had run, the water welled up gently, making a little mound like a clear, trembling jelly. It could no longer send up the lofty crystal column or let fall a crystal shower; it would never again command a rainbow. The water could not even find the voice to make complaint or talk of fulfilling itself to the limit of its capacities.

The Poet, the Woman
and the Wall

THERE WAS ONCE a poet and a beautiful woman; he was as radiant as noon-day, she dark and glimmering as a night sky where Venus partners the new moon. They had first caught sight of one another in the Court theatre when the poet was on the stage reciting his verses to the Archduke, and the woman sat in a box with her husband. From the moment when he looked up and saw her pale face gleaming among the shadows and she looked down into his, upturned in the rosy light, for each the world had narrowed to the person of the other.

They had snatched only a single meeting before the husband measured their mounting passion and confined his wife to a country estate. The poet came to live in a cabin among the surrounding woods, and every evening at the sunset hour they contrived to talk together through the lofty wall which divided them.

The agony of their separation was so great that it enabled the poet to write verses far beyond his earlier range, while the woman lived in such exaltation that she felt herself to be fleeting in the wind, putting out their blossom for the flowering trees, lying dark and still within the lake and yet also riding regally up it in the plumage of the swan. As for the song of the nightingales, it surged from her own heart.

During one of their dusky, wall-divided meetings, the poet noticed that on his side a stone had come loose, and he at once called out the joyful news to the woman. From that moment they devoted the whole of their time together to breaking a hole through the barrier: they no longer talked of art, of one another, of the hopes of their passion, but instead of how to prise out mortar, of where the woman should thrust her bodkin.

When they had loosened the last block which was preventing the young man from drawing his lithe young body through the hole it was after sunset and in a few minutes the woman would have to return to sit with her husband. So, most reluctantly, they prepared once more to put back the loose stones, concealing their handiwork. Before fitting back the last fragment, the poet and the woman gazed at one another through the narrow, dusty opening. Their eyes clashed like blades—the blue recalling the past day, the black presaging the descent of night —and as they struck together it seemed that some violent force cut through the universe, opened their breasts and exposed two quick, palpitating souls. Perhaps never in the history of the world have a man and a woman more nearly united. If the poet could have raised his imaginative fire by one degree, or the woman purged her receptivity of one grit, they would surely have fused and vanished into the world of spirit. As it was, when the poet sadly wedged home the remaining stone a white, wide-winged butterfly flew from the crevice and spiralled up into the dimming sky.

The next evening they went to the wall, their eyes almost blinded by the great red clouds of their desire. The poet leant his shoulder against the loose blocks, they fell inward and in an instant he was through the wall. Their eyes kindled, then suddenly were suffused with fear, faded and grew blank; the man still raised his arms automatically towards the woman, but she turned and fled back to the house. Her husband locked her in an ancient tower and set his oldest henchman on guard.

Every night the poet left his cabin, took down the stones and, greatly daring, crept to the foot of the tower to sing songs of his own composing. The woman experienced an even loftier exaltation than before as she felt herself to be driving across the heavens wrapt in the white bliss of the moon. The songs of the poet were his greatest, and are still heard today.

Land, Water and Wind

A STAG HAD COME down to the coast in order to lick salt from the rocks, and while his tongue slavered over the rough surface, his huge, melting brown eyes looked out to sea. To his astonishment the stag saw a huge body thrashing about in the shallow water of a bay. Full of fastidious curiosity, the deer picked its way round to the part of the low cliff nearest to the disturbance and stood there, beneath a group of pines, watching the struggle below.

At last, distinguishing two little eyes and a horribly serrated mouth, the stag called out:

'What are you doing there? Have you slipped and fallen into the water? If so, you can easily drag yourself out further round the bay where the beach is shelving.'

'Fallen into the sea?' snarled the basking shark. 'Of course not, it's the sea which has fallen away from me. But what are you doing perched up there on the shore? Has this cursed tide left you high and dry?'

'Left me high and dry; I hardly understand what you

mean. I have merely come down to the sea for my salt-lick. Naturally I live here on the land.'

'I don't think it is in the least natural. All natural life is in the water. Whatever you may say, I guess you have been stranded and now have been fuddled by breathing too much air. You had better jump back at once into this promontory.'

'Promontory!' exclaimed the deer. 'Promontory! Why, you are in a bay and I have just left the headland in order to look at you.'

'Crazy, got everything upside down and the wrong way out,' snapped the shark. 'All the same you'd better come back, because some day we shall see to it that the waves flatten the sea walls and flow all over the globe.'

'That is very ignorant nonsense. No doubt our continents would long ago have closed across the oceans if it were not that a supply of water for rain is necessary to us. The sea is nothing but a flux on which the outlines of the continents are drawn.'

'The outlines of the continents? Why, the shape of the seven oceans is all that counts. The land does nothing but fill the gaps, useless, filthy stuff.'

The shark lashed his tail angrily until the stag was splashed with salt drops, while the stag himself stamped his sharp hoofs at the cliff edge, spattering the big fish with soil and pebbles.

At that moment the pines began to sway gently, an empty cone falling to the ground; some wrinkles on its calm surface made a dark track across the bay. The combatants heard a whisper coming from the tree-tops:

'Listen, creatures of Land and Sea. Know that the oceans are happy to have the land to contain them. Know that the continents should rejoice that the water is there to draw their coastlines.

'Reflect on my plight. Because I have no boundaries but am free to blow for ever round this space-hung ball, I am almost without being. I am invisible and can only make my presence known by bending the vegetation or roughening the water; I can only speak with the lips of the leaves and the falling waves. Be thankful that each one's bay is the other's headland, for otherwise there would be neither bay nor headland; without the contending of one against the other, both would lose all character and virtue. I envy you infinitely, infinite——'

The whisper was hushed as the pines grew still again and the wrinkles vanished from the sea.

The tide had turned, and with an enormous heave the basking shark contrived to launch himself back into deep water; the stag trotted inland to rejoin his herd.

The Couple who Lived
and the Couple who Died

ONE FEBRUARY DAY when the sun had broken from its crimson winter cocoon and was shining with a pale promise of spring, and when the narrow sheaths of the snowdrops were letting fall their tear-shaped buds, a double wedding was celebrated in a village church. These young men and girls, so it was agreed, represented the best of their generation in all the country round: the grooms well-grown, intelligent, decently ambitious and with promise of a full maturity; the brides pretty, ravishingly fresh, gay and serious. All four had known one another from childhood, yet had been blessed with a sudden falling in love. John had fallen for Jessie (whose rippling hair he had admired since sitting behind her in school) when she returned from a visit abroad; William had adored Maggie from the moment when he had suddenly seen her through an open door and the scales of familiarity had dropped from his eyes.

The old clergyman who celebrated the marriages experienced a degree of emotion which had become rare with him as he pronounced a blessing on so much youthful sincerity and hope, such a tempting display of the fruits of life and so simple a trust in its promise. He who had seen the filling of many cradles and many graves found himself fervently praying that he might indeed be empowered to conduct God's blessing into these four lives.

The couples settled into their cottages and their happiness waxed and ripened. The young men learnt to be tender and satisfying lovers and the women blossomed as only well-loved women can, their gaiety and their seriousness intensifying together. Whether they were in one another's company or apart, each woman moved in the aura of her man as though clad in an invisible cloak.

The second summer after their marriage the two families decided to take a seaside holiday at the same small resort. Maggie had already borne a fine son, while Jessie was with child and was very ready to declare that the baby she was carrying for John would be the finest in the world. Just before they left for their holiday John was given a job that seemed to offer an opening into a golden future. Surely if ever human beings have been haloed, these couples went with a radiance about them during the summer days by the sea.

On their last afternoon the four friends walked down to the beach and lay in the shade cast by the lofty chalk cliffs; they were ready, even eager, to get home and press on with their affairs, yet were reluctant to leave a place where they enjoyed themselves so much. Presently Maggie persuaded William to go down with her to dabble their baby's toes in the sea. Jessie leant her belly against

John, protesting that she was too busy to move.

The parents were bent over their child, poking its toes into briny bubbles, when there was a roar more ominous than that of diving aircraft, and then a silence disturbed by cries which they found were coming from their own throats. The huge slide of angular blocks, cruelly white and pure, sloped steeply from the shade where they and their friends had been lying out into the sun.

After the burial service, the clergyman, by now very feeble indeed, did his best to comfort the weeping pair. 'Do not question God's design,' he said. 'I have seen the trajectory of many lives, I have experienced my own, and I am not sure at what point along it we should wish to be cut off.' William muttered something against religious cant, for it was impossible for either him or his Maggie to believe in old age and death. Indeed, deeply though they sorrowed for their intimate friends, they tasted the added zest in life which the death of others can bring. John's job went to William and every youthful hope seemed possible of achievement.

Many hopes were fulfilled, some withered, and a few more were dashed. They came to own a finer house than the cottages where they had been born; Maggie went up to London to represent the Women's Institutes and had glass-fronted cupboards filled with good china and plate. Each had become a familiar presence to the other; they anticipated one another's kindnesses, as also one another's failings and foibles. Maggie's eyes no longer sparkled when she looked at her mate, their love-making had become rare, hasty and insignificant. His wife suspected

William of having enjoyed one or two of the village girls, but of course she was too sensible to inquire. Their children were good children enough, but when the time came they married ordinary young men and girls. There were no miracles.

The seasons rose and fell faster and faster, or so it seemed to the ageing couple, though the springs were never as bright as they had been, nor the summers as warm and golden. All through the years Maggie had tended the graves of John and Jessie, and although after the first grief was gone it had become a habit, for a time almost an embarrassment, as she grew older a new emotion, a creeping nostalgia, took hold of her when she carried cut-flowers to the graves or tended the plants which grew there. So it was that when at last the moment of William's retirement came, she insisted they should go once more to the resort where the accident had happened.

The place had grown, had put out more red streets, more asphalt paths, shelters and railings. As for the old couple themselves, it was only a few surviving material things, such as the worn, cast-iron bollard on which they had photographed one another with a good deal of laughter and kissing, that enabled them for an instant to identify beings altogether different from themselves.

They toiled slowly up the cliff path, for the beach was too rough for them now that Maggie was stout and short of breath, while William had his share of the undignified ills to which old men are prone. They sat down on a concrete seat not far from where a gap in the cliff edge, fringed with sere autumn grass and thistles, still marked the place of the great fall. They stared out at the horizon and could summon no emotion of any kind.

A goldfinch alighted on the head of a thistle and rummaged among the fluffy seeds until the plant swung up and down breaking the line between sea and sky. They watched while the thistle came to rest and the bird sat uttering its little song, a gay harlequin of a bird in black and yellow with a crimson mask. There was a rush of rufous plumage as a hawk swung up from below the cliff edge, the extended talons closed, then bird of prey and singing bird had vanished.

The old woman nodded her head sadly as she stared at the vacant but still swaying thistle. She reached out for her husband's knee and the old man, whose afflictions were making him uncomfortable on the concrete, laid his hand on hers and stroked it vaguely. As he touched the dark, knotted veins on the back he looked at them half tenderly, half with repulsion.

The Three Women

A YOUNG GOD SENT a message to the city over which he was the presiding deity, saying that he wished to take a human consort. He ordered the citizens to pick out from among all their women the two who could be considered the most worthy of this honour. He would then make his choice between them.

After long debate the citizens selected two high-born ladies, Eudia and Thalpomene. As they were extraordinarily unlike, it was felt that the god should be pleased by either one or the other of them. To prepare the temple for the exercise of the divine choice, two alcoves were hung with curtains, the one of pure white linen, the other of deep crimson brocade. The first of these alcoves was furnished with a plain birch-wood couch, the other with a couch superbly carved and gilded, its feet shaped like claws and the raised end like the head of a lion.

When all was ready the citizens sacrificed and burned incense until the god descended into the temple, taking

his place on a throne before the alcoves. Immediately
the white curtain was raised by a young virgin, an
attendant of the temple, who stood there holding back
the linen to expose Eudia lying languidly on her couch,
her head propped on her folded hand. She had smooth
fair hair, her pale features were of extraordinary perfection and she was clad in a white tunic held by a
broad silver belt.

'What could you offer me, Eudia,' said the god, as
he sat admiring her beauty, 'if I took you for my consort?' She raised her head an inch or two, but still it
was drooping.

'I would offer you calm in our relationship and in our
house, for I would discipline myself and the household
with a dignity proper to my rank. You would never in
me find passions, moods or desires to upset your peace.
On the marriage bed I should be obedient, submitting
absolutely to your will for I know, my lord, that this is
one part of my duty. These are my promises and what
I promise that I will do.' She now finished with a trace of
the spite not uncommon in women of her kind, 'To turn
from the promised future to the past that can never
be undone: you will find the seal of my virginity un-
broken, a thing not always to be expected in brides,'
and her eyes turned towards the crimson curtain. As
her soft level speech ceased, she dropped her slightly
raised head back on to her hand and at this sign the girl
lowered the curtain across the alcove.

Next the attendant lifted the crimson curtain, reveal-
ing Thalpomene stretched on her couch in a flame-

38

coloured gown threaded with gold. Her own handsome
head, with its brilliant complexion and black curls, was
reared above that of the golden lion. She hardly waited
for the god to finish the question, which he addressed
to her in exactly the same words he had used before.

'I will bring you glory and exaltation,' she cried.
'With me your life could never sink to dullness and
tame domesticity. We will pursue unattainable ideals;
scale mountains whose tops are lost in cloud. Above
all I will bring you love; I will bring you ardour and
passion which even your divine potency shall not ex-
haust; and if it happens you are weary, then I will show
you that I am versed also in all the subtleties of love;
I will fan your desire until it leaps up once more.'

Already Thalpomene was leaning forward, her arms
open and her eyes bright, and one golden sandalled
foot was feeling its way below her gleaming skirts
towards the ground. The god motioned the girl to let
fall the curtain of the alcove. He sat for a moment in
meditation, then withdrew to his sanctuary, commanding that the rivals should appear before him there.
When the girl had led them to the steps in front of the
altar, the god rose and turned upon them the great
eyes that are a mark of godhead. His power went with
his gaze and assailed the women. Immediately Eudia
dwindled and hardened until all that was left of her
was a small silver ring lying on the altar; with a rushing
sound as though of wind, Thalpomene vanished from
the temple, but at her passing a fire was kindled on the
altar. The girl was left alone on the steps, and as her

eyes met those of the god she swayed where she stood. Commanding herself, she turned as though to look for her two mistresses.

'Stay,' cried the god, 'stay, my chosen consort.' The girl sank upon the steps, leaned her head against the sacred vessels carved upon the altar, and wept. 'Eudia did not please me, for what is discipline when there is no energy to restrain? Thalpomene did not please me, for what is passion without restraint? Confronted by the eye of Truth, one has dwindled into a simple outline, the other has vanished, mingling with the gases of the air. But you have withstood my gaze, for in you there is both passion and discipline. I was aware how when you first saw me your body flowered and your spirit was quickened, yet you carried through your task. Your name is Imagination, for in you energy creates its own form. Come with me and I will make you Goddess of the Arts of Men.' He picked up the silver ring and placed it on her finger and kissed her through the altar fire.

The Weevil and the
Chestnut Tree

THERE WAS ONCE a handsome, well-grown chestnut tree. A horse chestnut of the kind that has milky white flowers spotted with crimson. Ever since the first season when a pale spike had thrust its way upward from the flank of a fallen nut and a few rootlets had threaded their way downward into the leaf-mould, the tree had grown harmoniously from year to year. Now its form was full and massive with boughs opulent and bosomy in their curves; every May it was set with long white candles of blossom like a summer Christmas tree. Some loved it best for the flowers it raised up towards the sun; others for the shade it cast upon the ground.

When the flower buds were about to open one fine spring, a cunning weevil burrowed into the roots that writhed about like snakes in the darkness of the earth.

'Why do you toil down here in dull obscurity?' the insect whispered. 'Why are you content to grope unseen, endlessly seeking nourishment for the flowers? They have nothing to do but flaunt themselves in

41

the sun, yet all the admiration goes to them and their frilly petals. I shouldn't put up with such injustice if I were you.'

Then the long-nosed little insect tunnelled his way up below the bark, and bored a passage into the trunk, before he began to mutter:

'You are the backbone of the tree, the sole support of its whole structure; without you it would be as humble as a dandelion. Below you the roots have a lazy time lying about comfortably in the soft earth; above you the flowers have nothing to do but flaunt themselves in the sun and attract admiration. Why do you stand here hidden behind rough and dirty bark? If I were you I should see to it that my worth was recognized; I should consider it due to my pride and self-respect.'

Now at last the weevil ran along the branches and stuck his thin proboscis into flower after flower. The scent nearly made him swoon and the crimson markings dazzled his weak eyes but he murmured ingratiatingly:

'You most lovely and divine blossoms, I am sure that in the innocence of your exalted natures you believe that the rest of the tree is giving you of its best. In truth you are being betrayed. It might be thought that your sacred duty first to inspire the world with your glorious beauty and then to put forth the fruits of this great tree would win you the willing service of all those below you. This is not so, your Graces. If it were not for the shameful idleness of the roots lounging about in the soft earth instead of seeking your nourishment you could grow twice as large and remain in full beauty until the autumn. If it were not for the stiff-necked pride and stupidity of the trunk every one of you would bring forth a magnificent mahogany nut; none would fade without fruition or bear dwarfs and other abortions. I know how keen is your sense of *noblesse oblige* but I humbly suggest that it is now your duty to claim the full service that is yours by natural right.'

The roots drew in their capillaries and soon became dry and hollow; the trunk checked the flow of sap and rotted fast; the flowers tried to blossom so extravagantly that they were already sterile before their food supply failed. Meanwhile the weevil had returned to his mate in a snug little cavity just above the ground and they were breeding as fast as they could. Weevils thrive in dead wood.

Export and Die

THERE WAS ONCE a colony of penguins. They were ordinary unregenerate birds, much given to small sins. They stole from one another, tweaking away an attractive morsel of fish when a neighbour's back was turned; in the breeding season the males occasionally fought one another for the sleekest most agreeable females, while the females allowed themselves a fair ration of little wiles, gossip and harmless malice. It had happened once or twice within living memory that when a penguin was caught by one of the sea tigers that always lay in wait for them under the diving place it was generally believed that the victim had been pushed in by a rival. Still, on the whole, they were good, jolly birds enough. Although catching fish was hard and sometimes dangerous work, and although they had some bad seasons when food was short, the penguins found time to sit about idly preening themselves in the sun, to talk, philander and enjoy affection. Every day at dawn the whole colony assembled on the beach to do reverence to the rising sun. Perhaps they looked ludicrous bowing until their beaks touched the snow, and spreading out their stumpy wings. They were, indeed, rather absurd-looking creatures at any time. Nor, admittedly, did their dawn observance make any difference to the spinning of the earth or the burning of the sun; still, it was not a bad idea, giving them satisfaction of a kind and reminding them of the existence of things beyond their own very limited comprehension.

Normally the mated pairs produced a single egg and took turns at incubating (shuffling the egg gingerly from foot to foot between them to keep it from the ice), but sometimes a female might lay two eggs, discarding one of them, and sometimes a pair would be so idle or quarrelsome that they abandoned their egg. For these reasons there was always a certain number of surplus eggs which lay about until the gulls got them or they rolled into the sea. One day when most of the birds were either still incubating or busy feeding their fuzzy, voracious chicks, they were astonished to see a boat put into their bay. In it were two large important looking penguins with brilliant yellow collars above their white fronts, and a crew of small black penguins with little oars tied to their wings. One of the big birds came ashore, followed by members of the crew dragging a sack; he waddled with as much dignity as is possible to a penguin up on to a snowy eminence and, while his followers scattered some fine fish from the neck of the sack, addressed the colony through a megaphone.

'We come to bring you good news. In a distant coun-

try far beyond your reach penguin eggs are in great
demand. If you will give me eggs, I will bring you fish,
more fish than you have even seen at one time. You
will be able to give up fishing with all its dangers and
failures. You need never venture into the sea at all
except for pleasure. Bring out your eggs. Bring out
your eggs, and your fortune is made.'

Most of the listening penguins covered their eggs
or young, crouching over them and raising their beaks
in a threatening attitude until they looked like indig-
nant kettles. But a few males among the pairs which
had deserted their eggs edged up to the intruder and
fell into earnest talk. Before long the collaborators had
collected all the spare eggs and received in exchange
the big sack of fish. They held a last consultation with
the yellow collars, then while the boat rowed away they
mingled with their fellows, appealing to them singly
or in little groups.

I will not attempt to describe all stages of the slow
revolution in the penguin colony which resulted from
this first successful venture in export trading. Instead
I will be content to return there some years after the
arrival of the earliest yellow-collars in order to describe
the changed state of affairs.

The island and surrounding floes are now very much
more crowded—the number of birds must have doubled
or trebled. Indeed they are congested and squalid; the
graceful fringes of icicles formerly edging the cliffs of
rock or ice are now only broken stumps, while the
expanses of snow which once seemed smooth and light

as a soufflé are reduced to a grimy slush. There are droppings everywhere, and a stench of guano hangs in the moist air.

Although at four o'clock it is already nearly dusk and the season appears to be late autumn, row upon row of sitting birds are visible over all the level land surrounding the bay. Suddenly the whole place is flooded in a cold greenish light coming from lamps rigged untidily on poles. In this deathly illumination it is possible to see how the sitters are ranged back to back in long double lines with alley-ways between them; each bird is squatting on a pad of dirty sealskin with a tangle of wires running from one to the next. As the snow round them is melted it is easy to guess, what is in fact the case, that the pads are electrically heated. These birds are all females, and although they seem plump enough, indeed much fatter than before, their feathers have lost every memory of the gleam which Eros gives to free and lusty creatures. They sit in their rows, some listless with beaks sunk into their draggled breast feathers, the rest squawking, quarrelling and back-biting among themselves. It is no wonder they are fat, for every hour small black penguins bring round trolleys of fish and they can take as much as they want. If that is not quite so much as would be expected, it is because the fish is now always stale, every piece of it being imported ready filleted and then stored deep in ice caves.

Also every hour, between the visits of the fish-trolleys, other of the black penguin servitors patrol the alleys collecting eggs. Any sitter who has laid one presses a

47

button to light a small bulb on her electric pad which directs the attention of the collectors—usually emphasized by proud cries and waving of flippers. Some of the females, however, probably with unconscious memories from the days when eggs were laid only for hatching, try to conceal their products, for which reason the collectors are equipped with long-handled prongs for prodding suspects to their feet.

Once collected, the eggs are stored near the margin of the bay where they will be embarked as soon as the incoming boats have unloaded their cargoes of frozen fillets.

From what has been seen it might be supposed that in the new order the females fared worse than the males, having been turned into mere units of production. In fact the males were no better off. Isolated on the other side of a rocky ridge so that they should not be distracted by the sight of the females, the male penguins worked an electric generating machine. They worked in teams, shift after shift, to turn a huge wheel, the sole propulsive power being the press of their small webbed feet treading, treading on the slats. To generate the warmth and light needed for all-the-year-round egg production the wheel had to be kept turning night and day; the long summer days and the long winter nights.

In a secluded hollow, out of sight and earshot of the rest of the colony, the Managers had installed themselves with their families and a number of small black servitors. A few of the Managers were full-blooded yellow-collar birds whose superior size added to their general sense of importance; others were of intermediate size and hue, being the progeny of mixed marriages between yellow-collar merchants and the original collaborators. They lived in commodious chalets well warmed and lit by current from the main generator.

Such was the new order while it was at its most prosperous. The fish flowed in, coming from the boats, along the alleys, down the gullets and through the intestines into the eggs; the eggs flowed out, coming from the ovaries, through the Fallopian tubes, along the alleys, into the boats. All the while the wheel was kept turning, pressed by the small, black webbed feet.

Plans were just being prepared to introduce troupes of performing seals to amuse the sitters and turners in the monotony of their existence, when things began to go wrong. The Managers suddenly announced that owing to poor catches overseas more eggs would have to be produced for fewer fish. As a result, instead of being entertained by performing seals, the workers had to listen to harangues from Managers' deputies urging them to redouble their efforts to save the colony from ruin. The turners must strain to raise the temperature of the pads by two degrees and so help the sitters to reach their new target of two eggs *per diem*. Diagrams with symbols representing fish, eggs and penguins were drawn on sheet ice, and chatty Advisers went round giving tips on how to increase personal productivity.

Just when the heat had been raised a little and the more earnest females were laying two eggs every thirty-six hours, the Managers announced that there was now great difficulty in marketing the eggs as there was a glut throughout all circumpolar lands. Stacks of eggs accumulated all round the bay, and still less fish was disembarked. As the birds were becoming accustomed to contracting their stomachs and living with their cynicism, war was declared upon them simultaneously by two neighbouring penguin peoples. One of their foes asserted that their egg-dumping export methods were bringing it to ruin, while the other insisted that their withholding of eggs was the cause of its starvation.

The war was bloody and the colony defeated, for it was heavily out-numbered and had always been of a pacific temper. Indeed it would certainly have been annihilated had it not proved possible to make the two attacking peoples turn to fight one another. When at last peace was established the population of the colony had been reduced to just about the level it had held before the institution of the new order; the wheel was in splinters, the lamps fallen and the whole system of pads reduced to a charred tangle of skin and wires.

The Chief Manager emerged from one of the ice caves with the last case of fillets. He mounted a blood-stained rock and began an eloquent speech: he spoke of unique gallantry, of patriotism, of the longing of all to return to normalcy; he pointed dramatically to the wreckage of the production system and his voice rose high and impassioned as he offered to divide the last fillets among them if they would set to work to rebuild, to create a still newer order. . . .

A score of young penguins dived into the sea, splashing the orator from head to tail. When they emerged, with bright wriggling fish in their bills, I am sorry to say that several old females who were standing near seized the fillets and pelted the Manager on his white front and yellow collar. It was not an accident either that one of them upped with her tail and fouled both his feet.

A Woman as Great as the World

T HERE WAS ONCE a woman as great as the world. She was of a placid disposition, and, knowing everything, had no cares. Indeed, she would hardly have been conscious of her beautiful and complete existence had it not been for the visiting Wind who came to disturb her peace. He would blow round her where she lay, fluffing the clouds that lapped her idle limbs; sometimes he would caress her tenderly, his touch like that of a firm hand that feels the bone and quickens the flesh; sometimes he would blow stormily until her hair streamed out among the clouds. Always when he came he filled her mind with images of herself which hung before her and seemed by their mere presence to demand an explanation. She wished he would not come to trouble her, and when he did not come she hungered after him.

Sometimes, though rarely, he would arrive as a whirlwind, gathered together in a single rod, like a twist of molten glass. Then he would order her to open herself to him, and she would obey, to find her swooning consciousness sucked down into the caves and sea-beds of her being. After these visitations she would feel heavy, full of yawns and drowsiness, until at last she would part her thighs once again, allowing a new creation to come forth.

Perhaps her progeny would be fishes, many smooth and simple in their silver scales, others intricate with fins, barbels and spines; some delicate and lovely, their fins and tails like veils of iridescent silks; some ferocious and ugly with faces that were masks of anger. Or it might be a fantastic creation of reptiles, gigantic monsters plated and armed as though to endure the collision of planets; or birds, each species with its own songs and cries housed within it, its own skills in the shaping of nests, and plumage that was specific to the faintest bar on the smallest feather. All these creatures displayed in their every part the endless inventiveness, the immeasurably powerful imagination of the generating Wind; they became one with the Woman, increasing her beauty like a fine garment.

The Wind stayed away for a very long time; to the Woman it seemed aeons since he had so much as breathed along the channels on the back of her hand or stirred a single hair on her forehead. All her old reluctance to receive him had been forgotten; without him she was listless and lifeless; her beautiful body began to grow cold, to freeze and destroy its own life. Then at last the Wind was upon her—she heard his quick sighs and saw where the clouds were parting before him like a flock of springtime sheep. He butted through them and without caress or tenderness entered into her; all the particles of her vague knowledge of herself were blown together, given force and swept through her as though she were flooded by a pebble-laden wave.

The Woman was left sunk in her usual heaviness; indeed, it was deeper than ever before, while the images that came to her were more than ever clear and disturbing; she felt herself to be close to understanding the secret of her life. When the time came for the parting of her thighs she expected to give birth to a creation of surpassing wonder, to creatures stronger than the reptiles or more exquisite than the birds. When her womb brought forth ugly little mommets who walked clumsily on two legs and presently began to hang themselves with leaves and skins she was at first downcast; this progeny, surely, could do nothing to glorify and enrich her. But then the Woman was puzzled to feel in herself some new disturbing thing, a persistent self-consciousness as though the Wind were always with her, as though he were present among the tissues of her body. She began to be pleased by what had happened, thinking, with a clarity that before would have been beyond her reach, 'Now I am as clever and imaginative as the Wind; I can be his equal and no longer merely his obedient mistress—the instrument upon which he plays.'

Soon, however, she discovered that the new relationship did not suit her; she and the Wind were forever quarrelling; beating up terrible storms, floods, earthquakes and volcanoes in their anger. Some of their quarrels were provoked by the Woman's attempts to argue logically, some by her jealousy when she found that the

Wind liked to loiter among the new creatures, whispering to them and, she suspected, caressing them. Soon, too, the mommets themselves became troublesome. They tormented her skin and flesh in a hundred ways by their restless activity; they were spoiling her physical beauty even while they were destroying her age-long peace of mind.

Her quarrels with the Wind and her jealousy, her bodily and mental discomfort at length proved too much for the Woman's native idleness and good nature. Her body was her own and hers the completeness of being. She rolled over and over, she scratched and slapped herself, and as she scratched and slapped and rolled she began to laugh; laughed louder, altogether abandoned herself to laughter.

When she grew quiet and the clouds could again fold softly round her, she was at peace once more, knowing everything and caring not at all. She did not even care if the Wind never returned, being unable to forgive her for her wanton destruction. As any woman may enjoy the sight of her clean, warm flesh stretched before her in the bath with steam curling lightly from the pale landscape of the body, so she now surveyed herself appreciatively, heedlessly, as she rested among clouds.

Elopdatery

AMONG THE FROGS there were many laws and conventions; the oldest and one of the most harshly enforced was that against Elopdatery. It had been an important regulation in days when any infringement would have caused great social difficulties, but these dangers no longer prevailed. Conditions change even in ponds and ditches. Yet the punishment and opprobrium suffered by discovered culprits were more cruel than ever. This in spite of the fact that the least developed tadpole should have been able to see that the great dangers to the society of their time came not from Elopdatery and all that was related to it, but precisely from the opposite side of the frog character.

One day a delicately mottled young female, a creature whose every croak revealed the depths of her character, was convicted of the offence in question, and she and her accomplice, one of the finest young divers and swimmers of his spawn group, were exiled from all frog waters with the intention that they should perish miserably on dry land.

However, soon after the young things had been driven out with such unkindness, the very hate which had been directed against them helped to provoke the outbreak of war. As both sides made uncontrolled use of juice extracted from deadly nightshade berries, the entire frog people was soon annihilated.

Owing to the strength and devotion of the young male Elopdaterer which enabled him to carry the female overland on his back, the expelled couple were still precariously but happily surviving. He now bore her triumphantly back to their own pond from which corpses and poison had drifted away. They dived joyfully into the water and lived to beget a new race among whom the word Elopdatery was unknown. Without a name, the offence itself had ceased to exist.

The Woodpeckers
and the Starlings

THE PAIR OF woodpeckers were easily the most splendid birds in the Plantation. In spring and summer
their green plumage glinted with brassy lights, setting off to perfection the crimson crowns which were their
proud insignia. No other birds in the island, except the
kingfishers, had these tropical, metallic feathers; when
the sun's rays struck them they glowed and flashed as
though the yaffles carried rubies on their brows.

The other birds took pride in this princely pair; in
particular the garrulous nuthatches, who had been talking ceaselessly ever since they told Sigurd of the Treasure
of the Volsungs, regarded themselves as the retainers of
the larger birds whose habits and tastes their own resembled. Even the wrens liked to have them in the Plantation, though often when the yaffles flew laughing back
into the wood, the cock would whizz from an ivy-
covered stump and pour out more abuse than it seemed
possible for his morsel of body to contain.

As for the nightingales, they were confident enough of

their infinitely superior genius to feel an untroubled
appreciation of the yaffles. Returning from the South
where they had seen flamingoes, bee-eaters, hoopoes and
many other birds far more powerful, handsome or brilliant, these musicians moving softly among the thorn
trees enjoyed the bold eye and arrogant carriage of the
head, the showy plumage and even the strange harsh
voices of the natural lords of the Plantation. When the
male bird sang among the hawthorn blossom, whose pale
flowers answered the addresses of the moon, he was conscious of the crimson crowns now somewhere muted in
the darkness, and added his thought of them, as he would
have added a moss frond to his nest, to the shape of the
song which he built in the spaces of the night.

All the birds admired the woodpeckers not only for
their appearance and lordly ways, but also for their unique
skill as carpenters. It was a commonplace ability to be
deft in the weaving of twigs, moss, horsehair or cobwebs,
even if it were performed with the virtuosity of the long-
tailed tits, but it was a mark of extraordinary strength and
cunning to be able to carve a shapely chamber in the
heart of branch or trunk. By what means nature could at
once instil the idea of carving such a chamber and slowly
strengthen the bill to enable it to perform the operation,
no evolutionist has been able to explain. But the thing
had happened, with mathematical precision the yaffles
could drive a circular hole through bark and outer skin,
hollow a smooth cupola above it, and then drive down-
wards to make an oval cist with a couch of wood chips to
receive the eggs.

The first year they came to the Plantation the season had been already far advanced, and the woodpeckers had taken over an old, long-abandoned nesting-hole, cleaned out the cobwebs, made a small meal of the insect population, and succeeded in rearing a brood of four. Now, however, they were dissatisfied with this unworthy nest and resolved to cut a new one. The cock knew that some of his kind, ageing or decadent birds, were ready to work in rotten wood even though it inevitably resulted in a damp chamber and a ragged, unsightly hole. He would not imitate them; being at the height of his powers he decided to select the hardest wood which it was possible for any woodpecker to penetrate. He found an oak which, while it was outwardly quite sound, returned a note to his tapping that proved it to be slightly decayed at the core. The hen approved his choice and they began their exacting task.

For several days the Plantation echoed with their hammering, while a drift of chippings formed against the roots of the oak. When the work was finished all the birds rejoiced with the woodpeckers; blackbirds, warblers and finches, as well as the faithful nuthatches, flew beside them as an escort when they went to the largest and most populous anthill and there celebrated the end of their labour by devouring thousands of the piquant insects which swarmed on to their probing tongues. The nightingales did not join in this flight, but the cock sang one of his daylight songs, perched below the canopy of a young hazel leaf and with his eyes fixed on the perfectly round hole in the trunk above him.

60

It was while the hen woodpecker, now grown as serious and dedicated as a nun, was daily laying an egg on the sweet-smelling chips of her nest, that the starlings began to visit the Plantation. They came from the direction where a housing-estate for humans was spreading out from a small industrial town. At first a single pair, then three or four pairs together with a riff-raff of unmated birds roosted in the line of elms bordering the road. They were sleek and shiny as though wearing brilliantine, and they were always chattering together and imitating other birds or the noises they heard when picking up scraps round the human houses. One of them had accurately mastered the whistle made by local youths at the sight of smartly dressed young women. The woodpeckers ignored the newcomers, but they were aware that this particularly odious bird kept his loudest whistle for the occasions when they were flying past.

Their clutch was complete, and both the yaffles were as delighted and proud as the simplest minded chiff-chaff. Each of them in turn looked in through the hole to enjoy the white eggs gleaming dully in the gloom, faintly touched by such light as could make its way round their peering heads. Again the Plantation birds shared in the woodpeckers' satisfaction; surely now all was auspicious for their own nesting.

That same day when the cock passed their old nest he noticed straw sticking out of the hole and a dirty apron of droppings below it. Alighting on a nearby branch, he could hear an unpleasant din coming from inside and then, in response to his own angry cries, the squawking ceased, there was a scuffle and a dark head appeared in the opening. It was a starling. This bird looked into the fierce yellow eye of the woodpecker and made obsequious noises in his throat while at the same time uttering some shrill calls. Just as the woodpecker was about to launch himself at the intruder and split open his papey skull, a little flock of starlings arrived and settled on twigs and branches all round the hole. They chattered, squawked and stuck out their upper breast feathers in the fashion peculiar to starlings. Filled with disgust the great bird judged he could not engage in a dispute with such a rabble, and flew away feeling both scorn and humiliation. Admittedly he did not need the old nest and the starlings were acutely short of accommodation. Nevertheless, it was a defeat—a defeat by force of numbers.

Day after day the hen brooded the eggs, sitting in the narrow cell with her long tail folded above her head, while her mate, grown humble in the presence of maternity, fed her through the hole. When at last in place of the smooth convexities of the eggs she felt squirming soft bodies pressing through her breast-feathers her vigil was over and her hardest work about to begin. From soon after the hour of the dawn chorus until the owls began to call, the woodpeckers were the slaves of their young, whose funnel-mouths supplied insatiable bellies. On all their food-hunting journeys they avoided the distasteful spectacle of their old nest, but they did not suspect further aggression even though occasionally they noticed a starling or two hanging about near their oak.

The cock bird was weary and bored by the ceaseless

hunt for food, by the monotonous to-and-fro; his plumage and his sacred crown were growing dull from too much toil. How could the other birds be strengthened and inspired by his presence if he allowed himself to become dowdy and jaded? It was his duty to rest. He lingered for hours at the most appetizing of the anthills, shaking out and combing his feathers, feasting, and assuring himself that the sun was renewing the fire of his crown.

The hen too was tired; the vigil in the dark chamber had been a strain, and since their young hatched she had worked even harder than her mate. Searching for insects in a plantation of firs, she found the sun hot, the air resinous and soothing; after one or two journeys she settled herself on a comfortable branch. There she was lulled into a daydream, imagining the splendid future possible for their fledgelings (their quills were sprouting already) and rehearsing scenes in which she saved them from hawks by her bravery and cunning. The pine cones popped like passing minutes, but she did not count them.

The cock and the hen returned almost simultaneously to the Plantation, which by now had lapsed into the disillusioned melancholy of a summer afternoon. It was not peaceful, however. Both blackbirds from the nest in the hedge were flying up and down uttering their distraught ejaculations, the wrens were consuming themselves with angry song, and the whole wood sounded with the urgent speech of the nuthatches. With their heavy, looping flight the woodpeckers converged on their nest.

At their approach two starlings squeezed their heads out of the hole; a score of unmated loafers from the housing-estate stationed on neighbouring branches raised their usual hostile din. Scattered over the moss-grown roots of the oak were the bodies of the five fledgelings, their hopeful feathers showing through the down as ugly black stumps. One, lying apart from the rest, had been partly eaten and the flies were already massing. All five of the beaks, whose gaping greed seemed now so dear, were open in death.

The cock woodpecker hurled himself at the two silly heads in the opening, split one open instantly with his bill, and killed the second bird after a moment's struggle inside the hole. Meanwhile the other starlings gathered round outside, determined to mob him as he came out. There was pandemonium. The blackbirds and wrens were still shrieking and swearing, several woodpigeons dropped from the treetops clapping their wings, the nuthatches fearlessly attacked the starlings and found unexpected support from a pair of passing jackdaws hopeful of carrion. The hen bird did nothing but leap up and down in agony on a branch, alternately driving in and retracting her claws and uttering grotesque cries.

With the diversion made by the nuthatches and jackdaws the cock escaped and joined his mate, and the two great birds flew away together, their flight rising and falling in mournful unison. Their laughter, which sometimes had been mocking, sometimes triumphant, now, as it sounded through the wood for the last time, was harsh and despairing. Yet the clever whistling lout sent after them a shrill imitation of their cry. The bloody bodies of the dead marauders now lay with those of the young woodpeckers, and three other pairs of starlings, egged on by the loafers, were fighting for the hole.

It cannot be said that anything was at once outwardly changed by the going of the woodpeckers, yet the other birds were aware of some lessening of enjoyment in their affairs, some sense of a falling apart of the life of the Plantation. The nuthatches, the most deeply affected, plastered more mud round their hole for security and early fell silent. Even the starlings were annoyed when they realized that there was now nobody left who could make holes for their occupation. To justify themselves they babbled about equality and the evils of privilege. 'What was there, after all, in the least remarkable in the yaffles? They were large, and had bright feathers and red heads and a good deal of self-importance, all the rest was your imagination.'

'Of course it was,' replied the nightingale, 'that was the whole point.' And he sang his last lament, for the next season he and his mate did not return to the Plantation.

The Great Fish

IN A CERTAIN country there was a famous salmon
river. Starting from one of those dark mountain tarns
whose beds were torn out long since by the roots of
glaciers, it followed the usual course of such a river, hurling itself down the mountainside, sweeping through the
foothills, then moving in stately fashion towards the sea.
The salmon run had begun, a gleaming host of fish
forcing their way up against the torrent of the water—
force against force. They swam steadily through the slow
currents of the coastal plain, where the light was dimmed
by particles of mud, then climbed a weir beside a ruined
mill. As they struggled through the shallow slide of the
weir the salmon seemed like flying fish, for the water
rose on either side of them in flashing transparent wings.
The current grew stronger and more rough, sometimes
flowing taut and smooth over rocks, sometimes breaking
into foam. Again and again the fish had to leap rocky bar-
riers or flounder through the stony flurries of the river.
Among the many small or moderately sized salmon was

one much greater than the rest, dark with the experience
of many journeys through the oceans. So high was his
cunning, so tremendous the power of his lithe and finny
tail that when his companions had to make many little
jumps, or even wriggle through the narrow places, this
fish could always clear the obstacle with a single leap.
After these feats, when the lesser kind at last caught up
with him they would find him hanging in the shadowy
depths of a pool, motionless save for the slightest tremor
of his fins.

The throng of advancing fish grew fewer as one pair
after another decided they had gone far enough and chose
their territory. They would drop to the bottom and plough
troughs in the sand and pebbles; there, floating side by
side above the trough, the male and female would perform the strange violent ritual of egg-laying and fertili-
zation, the mingling of pearl-like eggs and swimming
clouds of sperm that are the properties for this small
underwater drama of creation.

At last the vanguard of the fish reached a point where
the river ran through the last hard rock stratum of the
mountain mass in a deep ravine. At the upper end it
formed a waterfall, for the greater part of its breadth
plunging over a rock face sheer and vertical save for a
few sharp projections from which the spray streamed in
white horsetails. The cascade, falling through the centuries, had worn a deep basin at its foot. Against the left
bank the remaining part of the channel was less precipitous, the rock stratum having split into a number of
steps, each with its miniature waterfall and basin.

Most of the fish found this barrier too formidable; some retreated and went up a tributary stream; some took possession of the gloomy deeps in the ravine. Still, a few were determined to go on, knowing there would be good feeding grounds in the tree-hung reaches above the fall. They tackled the ascent by the left bank, jumping from step to step, often swept back by the force of the torrent, but nearly all at last leaping triumphantly into the calm waters above.

Only the great salmon did not attempt to navigate the stairway; perhaps he was aware that he was too large to go that way, but it seemed rather that some reckless compulsion made him challenge the main waterfall, whose precipitous face must be cleared in one leap or not at all. For one evening and night the salmon rested in the pool, balancing himself at the point where the falling column striking down into the depths gently stroked and rocked his splendid body. Occasionally he rose for a fly, when in the dusk and under the light of the moon cattle browsing along the bank heard the curious soft slap of a torn water surface and saw rings spreading out with enough force to disturb the water plants round all sides of the pool.

Soon after dawn the salmon came to the top of the water and made two or three powerful turns, then bending his taut, steely body he leapt into the air, drops of water flashing about him like a cloak of sequins. The soft firm flesh struck the rock two feet below the sliding summit of the waterfall. There was a slight echoless sound from the impact of a yielding surface upon a hard one, then a silver shape a moment since proud and purposeful fell grotesquely back into the pool. Again and again these dreadful leaps were repeated; soon the perfect smoothness of the flanks was smudged with scars, and blood began to ooze between the silver scales. Sound and spectacle were alike horrible; it was anguish to think of a living body crushing itself upon eternal rock. The other fish shuddered a little, darted under rocks at every vain essay, their small souls filled with shame at the passion of their greater fellow. Yes, shame and awe came together inside their flimsy skulls.

The sun was well towards the south before the salmon sank to darkness of deeper water; his last leaps had missed the rim by two yards and more. At sunset it began again; the salmon made two or three more leaps, then seemed to gather all his strength. He swept round the surface of the pool in savage rushes, his tail forming little whirlpools at every stroke, then, with a most violent convulsion of his body, hurled himself upwards. He achieved the top of the fall; his eyes must have had a glimpse of the peaceful stretch of dark peat-stained water gently combed by hanging branches. With his fore fins working furiously against the water at the very point where it bent over the rock edge, he hung there for several seconds with the water gouting up in a crest above his head. All the smaller fish floated motionless, a little wishing for their champion to succeed, yet even more longing for him to fail—to be defeated.

They had their way. The effort was too great. The salmon could not gain any purchase for its tail, and at last the relentless unchanging thrust of the water pushed it back; it slid down the fall, struck one of the rocky projections and fell back into the pool. The body sank, swinging from side to side on a zig-zag descent as though a giant had dropped a spoon into a basin. After a short time it rose to the surface again, floating on its side, the whole of one deep flank with its pale underparts exposed to the sky. Either the spike of rock had severed the spinal cord, or the effort had been so great that the heart had burst.

The body floated downstream once more. It caught on rocks, was moved on again, twisted round, turned over like the piece of dead wreckage it was. At a bend in the river it was washed on to a spit of shingle and in a few hours had been picked clean by crows and starlings. A curving backbone like a coarse white feather lay on the stones.

Perhaps hardly more than a score of the other salmon had seen the struggles, the final fall, or the floating corpse. Yet before long the story had spread up and down the river and all the fish wondered at the epic. As years went by it spread far and wide among all salmon kind, and all the young fish were told it before they had two rings on their scales. The great fish that had challenged the waterfall became the source of awe, the object of wonder. As generations went by he became gigantic and was credited with golden fins, with eyes that burnt red in the darkness, and the power of sweet singing. So the fish who died became the one immortal.

Other Island

A SMALL ISLAND, temperate and fertile, supported a thriving population of beavers. They had been settled there for a long time, and had built and maintained a dam and lodge in the one river which drained the island. They knew of nothing beyond their own little domain, the unbounded ocean surrounding it, and a misty shape on the western horizon that showed shell pink at dawn and stood out black against the setting sun. From time immemorial the beavers had venerated this distant sea-mark, calling it Other Island and identifying it as both the home and the very person of Bea, their ruling goddess.

As the years went by, however, some of the most energetic beavers, the animals of action, came to feel restless and frustrated. They could find no satisfaction in the pleasant social life of the lodge, in aquatics, or in the beautiful myths and tales which had been handed on from generation to generation and which were the chief glory of beaver existence. They began to seek an

71

outlet for their energies in sea swimming, an under-
taking of great difficulty and discomfort for fresh-water
animals. They devised masks to keep the salt water out
of their eyes and mouths, and by a combination of
persistence and acts of real courage made journeys of as
much as five miles from the island. Their natural goal
was Other Island. When they were nearer to it by the
five miles that proved to be the absolute limit of beaver
endurance, swimmers were able to observe that it
appeared to be quite an ordinary island. There was no
sign of a divine residence or of any remarkable feature—
indeed as far as they could see it was both flat and barren.

Nevertheless, Other Island exercised a stronger and
stronger attraction on the beavers. Many of them gave
up all their old relaxations, their sports, story-telling
and idling in the sun; they also gave up earning their
daily fish: that is to say helping to maintain the dam and
lodge, and hunting. At first this neglect didn't seem to
make much difference to the beaver community, for
fish were plentiful and the buildings in good repair.
So the young males who had felt the lure of Other
Island devoted their days to devising ways of getting
there. Their mates thought they were mad and, after a
time, grew tired of saying that it was wonderful to be
left in peace.

The enthusiasts used their keen and expert teeth to
fell a huge tree of far greater size than any they had
ever tackled before, then set to work to hollow it. For
all their skill beavers are not shaped to use their teeth
like an adze, and so this task of making a dug-out boat

proved to be a long and painful one, leaving many of
them with very sore snouts. Still they persisted; they
were creatures obsessed. At great cost to their tender
noses they left two cross partitions amidships and lined
the space between them with clay, thus converting it
into a tank which they intended to flood and stock with
live fish. They also constructed benches along the sides
with holes above them, so shaped and arranged that
beavers crouched on the benches could thrust through
their tails and use them as oars. They named their
vessel *Ocean Tree*.

At last the Other Island Expedition was ready to
start. The whole population came to the river mouth to
see it off, and the Chief Elder made a long and high-
minded speech. In his peroration the Elder said how
great a thing it was that at last beavers were to set paw
on Other Island, how it would express the great
spirit of the race and how those who had perforce to
stay at home would send their hearts with the explorers,
experiencing with them every hardship and every joy.
The audience barked hysterically, thundering their
broad tails upon the ground.

The explorers beavered their boat, each one of the
rowers wriggling his tail through the correct slot and
clinging on to the bench with all his claws, while their
leader attached a wooden extension to the end of his
tail and hung it over the stern as a rudder. Then at a
signal from the steersbeast the whole crew raised their
tails as one beaver and rowed away at a rapid stroke,
their whiskers trembling with the strain. So they set

out on a journey of 500,000 paws—a journey, as it seemed to them, into outermost space.

Only one person was absent from the ceremony. This was an animal who had been the most gifted teller of tales, old and new, in the days when the beavers had more time to listen and enjoy. He failed to notice when the rest swarmed away and stayed meditating in the lodge; when he roused himself and found he was alone he swam off to do a little fishing.

A fortnight later the expedition returned; the stay-at-home beavers saw the vessel come crawling jerkily up the river, nearly half the rowing holes without a tail, and the survivors ragged of fur and emaciated. The welcome home was a little less enthusiastic than the send off, because during the past two weeks the absence of so many of the most active young males had led to a fish shortage, while there had been a serious collapse of the dam undoubtedly caused by the neglect it had suffered during the making of *Ocean Tree*. Still, most of the beavers went down to the river bank, and helped to support or carry their exhausted fellows back to the lodge.

When the worst cases of exhaustion had been put to rest and the others given a little food and first aid, the Elder made a short formal speech of welcome and asked the leader of the expedition for some account of the great adventure. The leader described the terrible strain of rowing, of using the tail in so unnatural a manner; he told of a violent squall which had nearly capsized the whole boat, but happily in the end had merely swept five beavers overboard. Then he spoke of the worst catastrophe of all; for reasons they could not understand, after less than a day's voyaging, the fish in the tank had begun to die and the explorers had been obliged to live on bad water and rotting fish. It was this which had caused the largest number of deaths in the party, and the most horrible suffering. However all sacrifice had been justified at last, for the expedition had reached its goal: beavers had explored Other Island. There was a murmur among the audience.

'And what did you discover there?' asked the Elder.

'Nothing,' replied the leader. 'You surely didn't expect us to bring back Bea in her fish-scale cloak or logs from her golden house?'

'Well then, what was it like?' said the Elder, nettled.

'You know Barren Point on the far side of this island? Well, it was very much like that but even more harsh and rocky. Indeed, two of the party died of thirst and fatigue while exploring it.'

The company applauded loudly, and more speeches were made proclaiming the triumph of beaverkind in reaching this farthest known part of the universe. During the tail thumping after the last of these speeches the Leader suddenly caught sight of the beaver who had failed to attend the farewell ceremony. The noise had disturbed his reveries and he was uncurling himself and looking about him in an uncertain sort of way.

'I say,' said the Leader of the Expedition, 'surely that beaver ought to show more interest? I'm not thinking of myself, of course, I was no more than an instrument.

75

But loyalty, you know . . . the honour of beaverdom . . .'

'I quite agree,' added one of the other explorers, 'he ought to join in. Why, it's almost an insult to Bea. . . .'

'Don't mind him,' the Elder answered reassuringly. 'As I expect you can remember, he is a great dreamer, and probably even now is far away, perhaps wandering in some magic land where the rivers are deliciously perfumed and flavoured, where the lodges stand for ever and are filled with music, where beavers are as beautiful as kingfishers. The banquet is now ready— or the nearest approach to a banquet that is possible in the present food shortage. When we have refreshed ourselves we will get the fellow to recite to us. I don't think you've had much experience of his powers. You'll be astonished how easily he can transport you to these strange lands of his. . . .'

And in truth the beavers listened far into the night.

Death and the
Standard of Living

THERE WAS ONCE a young girl who lived in a village with her comfortably widowed mother. She helped with the work in the house and the vegetable garden, and made the simple clothes which at that time she liked to wear. In her leisure she enjoyed wandering about the countryside, either by herself or with a chosen boy companion. She was hardly a beauty, but an extraordinary vitality inspired her face, and she was possessed of an aloofness, an ability to retreat into mysterious and private territories, that made her irresistibly attractive. She maddened the village boys by a frank heartlessness that was neither virtuous nor evil. She went to church and believed in God; she also sang in the choir for she was as fond of singing as of dancing.

When she was about eighteen a clever young schoolmaster came to the village, and it was not long before he discovered her to be not only desirable but also keenly intelligent. While he enjoyed her virginity and trespassed in those other secret territories of her being from which the villagers had been debarred, he was able at the same time to rouse her intellect and her ambition. Singing and dancing now appeared to her to be almost as foolish as belief in the supernatural; even the country round her home had become a little remote. Whereas before she had participated in it, now she observed and enjoyed it.

Though she kept her home in the village, with the schoolmaster's help the girl took a job in a neighbouring town. She earned good money, dressed nicely and went to have her hair done. She also went every week to the Public Library to take out books of metaphysics and philosophy. It was terrible to her to remember how recently she had lived without intellectual interests, had washed her own hair, and gone barefoot because she enjoyed the feeling of the summer dust pressed beneath her soles.

When she came of age she was as agreeable, well-disciplined and civilized a person as can be imagined, yet it was at about this time that the schoolmaster left her, going from her side suddenly, with hardly a word of explanation. Much of her distress came not directly from losing him, but from the loss of her own image of herself and her achievements which she could find only in his eyes. She moved altogether into town and took a more exacting and highly paid job. Having lost the love of God, nature and man, work became her distraction and the accumulation of material goods her obsession. She started courageously along this path and soon was as unable to retreat from it as the dinosaurs from theirs a hundred million years before. She worked harder and harder, and in her free time was too weary to undertake anything more strenuous than a visit to the cinema.

She spent all her money, the sole fruit, now, of her vital energies, upon possessions which she could wear, hang, pin or carry upon her person. While favouring tightly fitting clothes and shoes, she embellished them with beads, cameos, brooches and buckles; she loaded her arms with bangles and her ears with studs and dangling earrings; her hats were heavy with clips and ornamental pins; she wore one watch on her wrist and another on her lapel and often consulted and compared them, for she was increasingly aware of the passage of time. She invariably carried a gigantic and swollen handbag packed with cigarette cases and lighters, powder compacts, lipsticks, fountain pens and propelling pencils, notecases, money, business papers, memo pads and many other things of the moment and no moment. Although she had long ago ceased to have any religious feeling, she now added lucky charms and secret amulets to her other belongings.

As she advanced through middle life (and during that advance her body accumulated layers of fat) she felt the strain of so much work and the maintenance of so many possessions. As a result she began to fear death, yet was convinced that it was only her work and her possessions that held it at bay. She saw all her goods piled up to form a barrier between herself and the open grave which often appeared before her in imagination. As a girl she had liked to sit talking with the village sexton, but now memories of his shadowy, dank shafts where insects and young frogs fell and were trapped, cramped her mind with horror, and she toiled to raise her imaginary barrier higher and higher. She took to carrying a sling bag on her shoulder to take the overflow from her handbag, while yearly her hats were made larger to give cover to increasing flocks of hatpins. Her corsets were stout enough to show through her suits, yet in spite of them the seams of her jackets would often split if she made any unaccustomed exertion.

At last one day she fell into despair. She had long been working overtime and saving to buy a necklace of natural pearls, but now she had bought it the precious string gave her no more reassurance than the many artificial ones already belonging to her. Vague recollections of youth rose in her mind, competing with the image of death and the grave. They provoked a nostalgia so powerful and so agonizing that she determined to sacrifice her afternoon's work in order to visit the village of her childhood. Perhaps there she would find some salve more effective than the lustre of pearls.

As soon as she had stepped down from her bus into the familiar village street, the woman found her steps turned towards the footpath leading to a neighbouring hamlet— a hamlet which had been the home of her first childish sweetheart. She walked slowly and with pain, for she was fat and it was long since she had trodden anything but tar and concrete. Her beads and bangles tinkled with her paces, her stays creaked faintly, and she could feel that the amulet suspended in her bosom was swimming in sweat. She was weighed down by her hat, handbag and satchel, and by the umbrella and sunshade that proved her ability to plan for all contingencies.

The woman followed the old footpath as though by compulsion, an alien black figure moving through the meadows and below the elms. No longer was her consciousness free to flow out into the countryside; she could no longer even remember how once it had done so, how she had seemed herself to experience the stretching wing of the rook hung on the wind, or the nervous freedom of the hare wheeling away through the stubble. Consciousness was sealed off within the confines of her mind as closely as her brain within its skull and her body within its town suit.

She went forward through the mild autumn countryside in a mood of fear and nostalgia. Yet her eyes noticed the surviving landmarks of her childhood, the memory-fetishes with their load of associations. The contorted tree root, the two iron posts made glossy by passing hands, and the mounting block with its deeply foot-worn steps. The sight of a tall, straggling may-tree even reminded her of the excitement she had felt when she climbed it to reach an old magpie's nest and found inside a clutch of kestrel's eggs, smooth and warm within the blackened thorns. She did not remember, however, that feeling the eggs with her fingertips she had thought how from these simple shapes fierce hawks must spring with all their complexities of feather, organ and bone, and had wondered whether the whole universe of stars and men was but a greater embryo. This she had forgotten.

Nearly exhausted, the woman approached the stile dividing the two parishes where her sweetheart had been accustomed to meet her and to part from her. It was now

G

that her fear mounted and darkened within her, blotting out all other sensation. She had seen that on the far side of the stile a young girl was coming towards her; step by step they approached one another, converging as figure and image converge upon a looking-glass. The woman's range of vision was narrowed to the girl; fields, hedgerows and hedgerow elms existed only to display this child in her blue cotton frock. She was barefoot and her hair, free of slide or ribbon, fell carelessly about her mischievous, innocent and secret face. The woman experienced that cold contraction of the skin that comes when the spirit is touched on the quick. The pads of her fingers could feel the touch of the rough blue cotton; the balls of her feet renewed their contact with the beaten mud of the pathway.

Nearer and nearer they came; to the woman it seemed they were both imprisoned under a glass bell where an irresistible current drew them together. Now she saw only the girl's face advancing to meet her own; it was enormous, and every line and shade was intensified by a bright nimbus. Sometimes in the cinema she had longed to thrust herself into the picture, and had imagined the shock of impact with the taut, resistant screen. At this moment, as she struggled to raise her heavy body on to the stile, she expected such a rebuff, but there was nothing to check and throw her back: she was looking into a face as insubstantial as a rainbow, and through it showed the earth-dug grave, the black rectangle whose image had terrified her for so long. There was nothing to divide her from it; already the rainbow face was dissolving and

her body was weighted with its load of possessions; its
fibres, metals and glass.

With a last rattle of her beads and bangles, her earrings sounding in her ears, she tumbled into the pit. The
great velvet hat with all its sharp furniture was pushed
over her face; umbrella and sunshade lay across her
breast and hips, and her handbag burst open to scatter
more of her vain belongings into the grave. As compact,
lipstick and a shower of coins came to rest in the crannies
of her person and clothes, the first crumbs of earth began
to dribble down.

The Garden Seat

THERE HAD NEVER been a proper seat in the garden, and so at last, in a country sale, they bought one. It had recently been repainted white, and it was quite a nice piece of work, solid and well-shaped. For protection against wind they stood it in the sunken rockery, where it blocked half the path, necessitating a slight detour. For further shelter an embankment was made at the back of the seat, and for prettiness' sake they planted yellow alyssum along the top of the bank.

It looked attractive in its new white paint. Occasionally someone would sit on it to read or write, or a child would use it as a boat, but none of these things happened at all often, as it still seemed much more natural to sit on the stone steps, to lie on the grass and to go sailing in a construction of deck-chairs.

After the first year the long grass on the bank began to poke through the slats of the back, and the alyssum, a vigorous and fast-growing plant, to hang down over the centre of it. By July it was only possible to sit at the ends;

towards the middle the plants tickled, and it was a pity to crush them. Starting with coin-like pieces over the knots in the wood, the paint flaked a little then cracked along the lines of the grain. Before being painted white for the sale, the seat had been green, and before that again it had received a coat of brown varnish.

In the autumn the bullfinches came to eat the alyssum seeds, of which they are passionately fond. It was a fine sight to watch the cock bird, his breast glowing like the winter sun, as he demolished the seed sprays with his powerful bill. Husks showered on to the seat below, while the droppings of the bullfinches discoloured the remaining paint. During the winter a mole pursuing worms into the bank humped up a large hill of earth against the slats.

By the next year nobody cared to use the seat. A tremendous crop of alyssum seedlings had taken root beneath it and thrust up through the slats, while the old plants were very thick indeed and left barely enough room for an exceptionally thin person or a child to squeeze against either arm. Ants had colonized the mole-hill.

At the present time the seat has almost disappeared, but everyone still has to make a detour to get round the place where it was. As a matter of fact, it sticks out more than ever, and it looks as though in another year or so the path through the rock garden will have become quite impassable.

The Unites

THE BEING OF God quivered from a sharp point of experience; it was as though a gad-fly had bitten the flank of a horse and sent ripples coursing along the silky skin. He addressed a messenger, one of his creatures humble enough to be able to interpret the facts of the material world.

'Something is stirring once more in the region which you once reported to me was dominated by the planet Earth. There has been a long period of quiescence there; it is long since it gave me any further understanding either of joy or of pain. But this planet, which you reported to be the merest speck of matter, has enriched my consciousness; I keep in the hollow of my hand all the gifts I received from the working of its life. The exquisite designs that rose into my vision; the shapes as fine as snowflakes that came and went to my infinite delight; the trajectories of pain and joy that appeared before me like comets; the sparks of beauty that rained across the horizon of my awareness. How often do I turn them over in the depths of my contemplation. You went to observe for me the source of so much experience.'

'I did, my Lord. Once before I had been on a mission to that planet, but at your command I made a second journey there, guided by the light of your intuitions; for a second time I accustomed myself to earthly ways, to its limitations of time and space, and lived among the race of Men, for I found it was this new race of living things which had contributed to your Being. I lingered there for several centuries, by their reckoning, before I was ready to translate what I had learned for your understanding.'

'You told me first of all how some of my own consciousness had become concentrated in these Men in such a way that, through the material medium of the flesh and the special forms imposed by the cruel limitations of time, they could add to my being and my awareness. Then you described how this *spirit* as they called it, incorporated in each one of them, manifested itself in the material world. You told me of their music and poetry, their representations of nature which were surely the source of the shapes which delighted me; you tried to explain the feeble flickering reason of the Men which had sometimes illuminated and often vexed me. You gave me the history of whole societies developing in time which had appeared before me in those bright trajectories, while, at the other extreme in their human scale, you made me understand the passionate and tender loves of the males and females who together make up this race of **Men**, the loves which sparked so brightly in my sight. Perhaps, of all your tales, it was this last that pleased and exercised me most. I could not have supposed that a single animal species, made up of such transitory grains of life, could have contained within itself such tension, such subtle polarity, that the passion between them could reach my consciousness, much less that it could melt into a tenderness uniting it with the universal coherence of love. And be assured that if the love of these men and women penetrated my experience, then I also entered into theirs: in those moments they had intuitions of my being.'

'They had, my Lord, and they fed on their remembrance of it until the flesh began to wither. While it lasted the isolation of Man was assuaged; they could feel their life flowing back into that of the Earth on which they live.'

'You created for me, too, images of that material world, their planetary matrix. Of its rocks and waters, its vegetation that breaks into brightly coloured flowers and fruits; of the birds and the animals closely related to Man, with bones like his bones, yet without inspiration. It seems inspiration must long have forsaken your Men also, for they have dropped from my consciousness and I have filled my hand from other realms of being. But now again feeling and imagination are reviving upon Earth; when I sink into contemplation their shapes rise into my vision. I command you to return to that planet in its cranny of the material world and again to bring me news of the source of this experience, even while I meditate upon it.'

The Messenger made the necessary preparations to fit himself for life in the material universe and set off as a traveller familiar with its mazes. Much of the time he slid through days of blue space, sometimes azure, sometimes midnight blue, sometimes with flaming planets that blotted out all sight of other heavenly bodies; at others moving through darker regions where the stars slipped past one another as he went and the pale marblings of nebulæ strengthened and grew faint again, seeming to drift like morning mist. At last he entered the system of the sun and rested in the night shadow of Venus while he still further narrowed his faculties and his being ready for life on Earth, forcing himself into the straitest limits of time and space. He saw the planet as a bright star shining among so many others and could hardly credit that he would find it the cool, substantial place he remembered; how could there be fleshly life on that point of fire?

As he made the last stage of his journey he thought of his first visit to Earth when he had been sent there to account for the strange, blind unmathematical energy of which God had been made conscious. He had found the land masses and the margin of the ocean in possession of gigantic creatures, great cold-blooded monsters that nevertheless fought and coupled with the awful ferocity of biological life. This had been his first encounter with life. Then when he returned he had found the monsters gone, nothing remaining of them but a few petrified bones, and instead Men were in command, Men who were still full of the ferocity of the beasts but were so plagued by consciousness that their existence was one of ceaseless internal struggle. They fought and they loved and prayed; they tyrannized and were mild and charitable; set up glorious ideals and offended against them; created and destroyed. In God's hand suffering and joy, failure and success were equal parts of the treasures of his Being, but the Messenger had come close enough to Men during the centuries he had remained among them to understand something of their anguish, their wish for peace. Now, as he saw the continents begin to take shape among the oceans, he wondered whether he would still find men living upon them, or if, like the monsters, they would have vanished, leaving their little turning globe. He steered for land, its details began to emerge: there were fields, there were buildings and tracks, though fewer than before it seemed to him. Men were surely still on Earth.

The Messenger was once more present within the consciousness of God telling the tale he had brought back from Earth. In accordance with God's wish that his experience, his understanding might be extended to the utmost, the Messenger gave his story all the human verisimilitude he could command, for through the detailed images of his speech God could find delight even in the trivialities of the material world.

'I dropped on to a cheek of Earth just as it was turning into the shadow, at the hour, that is to say, which Men call dusk. As I came to rest on what appeared to be a small rocky outcrop among fields, I was presented with an enchanting scene, one of the few beautiful spectacles

which I was to see during my stay upon the planet. A
stream of pale twinkling lights was approaching through
the air, a veritable aerial river of light. At a certain point
it began to wheel round toward some massive black
rectangles which showed in silhouette against the dusky
sky, and as it wheeled the stream changed from white to
a deep crimson colour, deeper even than the heart of
a winter sun; the whole, therefore, was like a great bow
in the night sky, half glimmering silver, half incarna-
dined.

'I saw the stream beginning to dwindle, and cut short
my enjoyment of the sight to transport myself towards
the dark rectangle which was engulfing it. As I had
guessed, this represented the outline of a colossal building,
and my arrival at the entrance coincided with the tail
end of the aerial stream of lights. Looking up at it I
was for the moment convinced that the human species
had indeed been superseded and that I was now at the
hive of some kind of insect, enormously increased in
size since my last visit.

'In the air above me there was a cloud of winged
creatures with gross bodies, skins that gleamed dully in
the lights, huge glassy eyes and antennae or feelers
projecting from the head. Each had a white light in the
forehead and a red one on the back, but even this did
not convince me that they could not be insects for, as
you will recall, both glowworms and fireflies carried
lights. However, when I penetrated the opening between
huge sliding doors where all these creatures, having
alighted, were jostling one another in a kind of blind

haste to get into the building, I began to doubt my first impression. I saw that they were indeed covered by a tight-fitting skin, red, shiny and unpleasant to the touch, and that a similar membrane stretched between their fore and hind limbs, but I observed that these skins were fastened with mechanical seams, and each creature on entering the hall extinguished his lights, disconnected his antennae, slipping them into a breast pocket, and then opened a valve which allowed an escape of gas and a sudden deflation of their gross-looking bodies. The illusion of gigantic eyes was caused by plastic lenses worn like goggles attached to the close-fitting plastic caps. These lenses served partly as a protection for the eyes in flight, partly to ensure that the Unites should view their surroundings slightly magnified. As for the faces themselves, when seen without the caps and goggles which half concealed them, they were unmistakably human in feature, yet there was a monotonous similarity between them, due more to expression than to actual physical identity. There was a total blankness in their eyes as though there was an opaque skin behind them; they had neither the steely vitality of wild animals nor any trace of the mysterious mark of personality which was the glory of the human face as I remembered it. This vacancy of expression was enhanced when all these creatures put lumps of some substance into their mouths and began to chew as they moved off to stand in long lines waiting for lifts. The patient, empty eyes, the steadily moving jaws recalled to me neither men nor insects, but rather the cows which on listless summer days used to stand in their meadows chewing the cud, oblivious of everything beyond the pestering flies.

'I began now to allow my perceptions to turn towards the building itself, although I formed only a hasty impression of it, with no understanding of the way in which, as I shall presently describe, it was integrated with the lives of its inhabitants. The gaunt opening with its sliding doors gave straight on to a large central hall which seemed rather to be the base of a shaft than a room on its own account. Above the ground-floor level it was bounded by tier after tier of balconies, all made of the same rough-faced substance, some form of concrete, coloured a dullish red. I could see long lines of doors giving on to these balconies along which crowds were shuffling as they were disgorged by the lifts. On ground-level some effort had been made to give an impression of architecture. The walls were lined with plates of red glass decorated with cog-wheels stencilled in black. At the inner end was a huge niche occupying the whole wall. At first I thought it contained a crucifix, which, as you will remember, was one of the strange and poetical forms in which Men used formally to express confused inklings of your Being. A generalized figure stood in the middle of the niche with arms outstretched at shoulder level. But there was no suffering, no feeling of any kind in this figure; merely passivity; the blank eyeballs stared straight out towards the sliding doors. Then I observed that beneath each horizontal arm, and these were elongated a little beyond normal proportions, there stood a line of figures all of identical height and appearance, and all gazing over their shoulders towards the central figure. Beneath this lifeless composition the word EQUALITY was written in letters of red glass. In the centre of the hall, much rubbed and chipped by the crowds daily surging around it, was another piece of sculpture, this one in the ground and of such complete naturalism that one might suspect it to be formed of real people dipped in a concrete wash. It showed three figures, clad in the tight-fitting skins I had already seen. One, coloured red, carried a cog-wheel, one, a bright pea green, held a large cabbage, while the third, a sober black, carried a book, evidently a ledger. Each rested his free hand on the crown of the head of his left-hand brother in the trio. On one side of the concrete pedestal was inscribed: To All Unites For Ever; and on the back, in quotation marks, "Unites The Human Race"; both inscriptions were so much worn as to be almost illegible. This was my first intimation that these creatures, undoubted descendants of the Men whose experience you contemplate, now called themselves Unites, and that this race was universal all over the globe of Earth.

'I dwelt for a moment before this group allowing the whole scene to sink into my consciousness. The shuffling crowds of Unites, their jaws swinging monotonously, the rattle and whine of the lifts, the footsteps echoing along innumerable balconies and corridors, the slamming of doors like distant machine-gun fire, all of it enclosed in this vast shell of ill-finished concrete with its gaudy red glass panels and glaring fluorescent lights. Then something further penetrated my consciousness, something I had not observed after so long an absence from Earth. None of these Unites spoke more than a rare monosyllable. The footsteps, the lifts, the banging doors, and, as I fancied, a faint sound of chewing, were the only sounds in the hall. So oppressed was I by the ugliness and sheer dullness of this interior (of which, Lord, I can give you no comprehension so far is it removed from the realms of your experience) that I determined to withdraw my presence before nightfall. Almost as soon as I had exchanged the green light of the fluorescent tubes for the Earthly night with its marvellous view of many stars and planets, the doors rolled together and closed with the sharp clap of automatically controlled wards dropping home. The block was perfectly dark, not a ray of the glaring light I knew to be enclosed within its shell could escape into the outer world. There were no windows, no opening of any kind.

'I was comparing this pile, and the others which I could perceive across an expanse of concrete, with my memories of the great buildings put up by men in former times, their cathedrals, castles, palaces and follies, when to my surprise I saw a single flying form against the sky, evidently coming from one of the other blocks. The silhouette was identical with those of the Unites, but this lonely flyer carried no lights and was evidently making away from the colony towards the outcrop where I had alighted. I allowed him to accelerate and leave me far behind. When I reached my former resting place among the rocks there was no sign of any living thing.

'Indeed this lifelessness was one of the changes I now

noticed; there were no owls nor any stirring of the small wild beasts which used to survive even in Europe, and when dawn came, still silence, no single song from the delicious chorus of birds which had greeted my former dawns upon Earth. This chorus distinguished the season of love, and was the unconscious, innocent counterpart among the birds of the passion between men and women which has given you such delight. Such things as this, Lord, lack the power to penetrate your consciousness, but yet perhaps add some light, some texture to your total Being.

'Now day broke and dawn came without a sound, until suddenly the most hideous wailing sounded from the direction of the colony and I looked towards it in the brightening light. I could now see that there were three of the enormous concrete blocks, such as the one I had visited the night before, and a fourth one considerably smaller, all facing on to a huge concrete-covered square. One was coloured pink and had stencilled upon it dummy figures of increasing size, suggestive of a growing child; the second was dull red and bore the stencil of a cog-wheel like those which I had seen in the glass panels inside it, next to it was a bright pea-green pile charged with a cabbage. The smaller building was itself black, and its badge, an open ledger, was marked upon it by exposing the rough concrete of the walls. Attached to a small projecting wing at the rear was a tall chimney, the only one in the settlement. Lying at some little distance from these saturnine, yet shoddy tenements, was a large circular construction recalling what I remembered as a bull-ring or sports-stadium though with much higher walls; it was painted in a monstrous style with zig-zags of blue and orange. Farther away again, in the direction from which the stream of Unites had flown the night before, I could distinguish a compact cluster of low sheds and other evidently industrial buildings. As the morning light flooded the countryside and allowed me to see to the horizons, I found I was in low undulating country of the kind I remember in the English Midlands, but the hedges and woods of earlier days were gone, and instead all the land was divided into equal plots of some ten acres enclosed by wire fences, and each supplied with a concrete hut bearing a number. On all sides (for my outcrop gave me a wide view) I could see the silhouettes of other Unite colonies, all with the four tenements, the stadium and factories. I wondered in that moment, Lord, had they levelled the mountains, had they filled in the seas?

'As I was scanning the points of the compass, trying to estimate the number of these clusters, the sirens on the neighbouring roofs renewed their undulating wail, the sliding doors of the three large blocks were levered back and swarms of Unites emerged who had evidently been packed behind, waiting for the spring to release them. From the Red Block Red Unites came, queued to mount a raised platform and took wing in the direction of the factory; the Green Block disgorged Green Unites who flew in more open formation and settled in fours on the smallholdings. At the Pink Block the response was rather more varied. Pink Unites certainly appeared, but some of them emerged pushing little trucks filled, as I could see, even at this distance, with infants, and stood them in rows in an enclosed parking place, while others formed small contingents and marched towards the smaller black buildings where a single door gave admittance, but no one came out.

'While I was still absorbed in this, my first experience of the unvarying events of the Unite morning, with which in time I was to become so sickeningly familiar, I heard voices quite close at hand and seemingly coming from below ground. You will understand the strong emotion which surged through me when I again heard human voices, talking with life and feeling, a proof that this elusive and impermanent instrument was still in being, could still serve you.

'My perceptions, quickly guided by this most stirring sound, saw how, between the sheer face of an outcropping rock and a boulder, there was a dark entry only partly screened by a dwarfish thorn tree. There stepped out from it a Unite dressed in the standard shiny green skin, but the cap and lenses pushed back allowing me to view his face. To my delight I saw in it many of the traits which had become most dear to me in the human race as I used to know it. Above all there was at that moment in his eyes both a light and a shadow, as though he had just experienced some revelation too great for his understanding. His eyes prepared me for what was to follow. There stepped out after him a young girl, and the grace with which she moved through the rocky opening made me more aware than I had been when I

98

was watching them, of the wooden lifeless movements of the Unites. She had loose chestnut-coloured hair and a cloth of a darker shade of red-brown was twisted round her waist; otherwise she was naked. The girl took the Unite's two hands and as she raised them the shiny membrane of the wings was partly unfolded, making still more striking the strange contrast between the man in his plastic envelope, so hideous in colour and texture, and the girl with soft coarse cloth against her skin—a sight which in itself could delight and inflame the senses. As they dropped their hands such a charge of emotion ran between their eyes that surely you must have seen it and known that significance was indeed returning to Earth.

'The man pulled on his cap, and the lenses came down before his eyes cutting him off from further traffic with his beloved; then I saw him slip down beside a spur of rock and presently appear on a neighbouring allotment where, as I now noticed for the first time, there were only three Unites at work instead of the two couples to be seen on all other plots as far as sight could reach. He went to the concrete hut, fetched his hoe and went to work beside the other three, who appeared to take no notice whatever of his late arrival.

'From what I had experienced I did not doubt that unknown to myself you, my Lord, had guided my flight and caused me to alight at precisely the point on the globe of Earth from which came the flashes of feeling and imagination which had once more disturbed and delighted you. I decided at once to penetrate the cave where the girl had now retreated. As I made my way down towards it, I discovered that on one side a long grassy hollow, screened from view beyond a miniature precipice of rock, gave pasture to half a dozen sheep, among them some milking ewes. Each animal was tethered by a harness and cord of plaited wool securely pegged into the ground. I was happy to notice some thyme and even a few harebells growing in the grass among the ancient rocks, enough to prove that there were survivals from the wild life which had been one of the small especial pleasures of this planet.

'The fissure proved to be narrow and much obstructed both by fallen blocks and sharp projections. The inmates, I reflected, were probably living there secretly and had need of an obscure approach; on the other hand I was already convinced that the cow-like habits of the Unites, their dulled senses and lack of curiosity, would make it easily possible to live among them without arousing suspicion. For all their lenses, dullness would make them blind.

'When daylight had almost been left behind I found the rocky passage was closed by a leather curtain, and as I pushed beyond it I came suddenly upon a spectacle which astonished me, even though after so short a time on the Unite Earth my expectation of the probable had not as yet hardened. Here folded in the depths of the rock was a strange scene of the rich and exquisite set in the roughest matrix. The cave was lit by two hanging lamps and for the most part their modest flames served only to darken the angled recesses of the rock, but here and there they struck veins of white quartz and made them sparkle. These crystals had been formed in terms of earthly time very long before even my first visit to the planet, when upsurges from its boiling inner layers had melted and fused the ancient stones. At one end in a natural alcove where the crystalline veins were at their richest, there was a rocky shelf furnished in such a way that I was at once reminded of the altars fumblingly raised in your honour by earlier races of men. On one side of the shelf was a small pile of books, a few of them in brown leather bindings, the rest in faded cloth covers of a later age; on the other side lay a sword in a jewelled scabbard. Between books and sword there stood a footed cup or chalice of shining metal enamelled and encrusted with pearls. Here was the first and last object, my Lord, which I was to recognize from my earlier visit; it was a famous royal cup which after many adventures came to rest in the British Museum in London, where I had often seen and admired it. Above it, suspended on woollen strings from staples driven into the naked rock, there hung a many-pointed crown, a golden crown, a crown of royal kings. It was a glorious example of one of those headpieces first designed to symbolize the sun in the days when you were worshipped in the guise of that star, but which later were worn by monarchs who claimed to rule their people in your name. As the lamplight fell on the crown it burnt as though a miniature sun were indeed rising or setting in the cave; each of the rubies clasped upon it glowed deep red like a swollen and dying star.

'The other furniture was of the roughest sort, yet
with the true quality of things which men shape for
their own needs. There was a wooden table, three stools
and a couch covered with sheep skins, while a second
curtained fissure led into inner recesses which I guessed
would be sleeping-places.

'This was the furnishing of the cavern, and if, Sire,
you have granted me the power to give you a true
apprehension of the quality of the place, you will understand how my earthly senses rejoiced at the contrast
with the only other habitation I had as yet seen, the
Unite tenement. Compare with that dead, shoddy flat
monotony far more lifeless than the tomb, this hidden
fastness! Here the walls were patterned and shaped by
the long processes of earthly time, the light moved with
life and was echoed a thousand times in the crystal
facets on the walls; the texture of wood, fur, cloth, gold
and precious stones had each its own suggestive quality,
and in the soft light their colours achieved a harmony
subtle as that of a butterfly's wing; all were the products
of individual men and women. To add significance to
this profound sensuous satisfaction there were the books,
the sword, the crown and the cup to express the blind
intuitions, the symbolic imagination of the men who
served you so well, my Lord, in time past.

'But I have described the stage without the actors. It
was strange to me that all night these creatures of flesh
and blood and bone had been folded in the rock below
me, and I had not known that they were there. The
young girl had already returned to her stool, picked up

a distaff and begun to spin; not far from her an old man sat at the table in a loose robe of dull purple cloth, tightly belted. He might have served as a model, Sire, for that Englishman whose genius participated so often of your spirit—for William Blake when he drew his Ancient of Days. He was reading and his whole body was perfectly still yet seemed to be full of movement as though he had the strength to give rest itself some positive force.

'Though confined within its walls, neither the old man nor the girl was, I knew, inwardly present in the cave, for their minds were ranging farther than nest-building birds; the third being was wholly there, an alert presence in his own corner of time and space. A large negro lay on the couch, his muscular limbs denting the white fur of the sheep skins. He stared at the girl and, seeing her still a creature of love, cheeks and eyes glowing and her whole person enveloped in that alluring and yet impenetrable aura of recent passion, he smiled mockingly, humming some love-song in time to her spinning. As I observed the twist of the negro's lips, mocking perhaps both the girl and himself, I thought how humour is the one human gift in which you can never participate, for your Omniscience cannot know man's sense of the incongruous.

'Looking at the girl I found myself thinking of her lover. How extraordinary must be his emotions. He could enter this place, rouse and satisfy a woman, then return to the lifeless Unite world. The cave would, I supposed, seem to him to be his reality and he would move among his swarming fellows in the tenements and on the allotments as though he were a dreaming stranger. Perhaps after all, I reflected, his position would not be so very different from that of the great artists I remembered living in the ordinary society of the past.

I determined my next duty must be to observe the lives of the Unites, not merely to discover to what pass the human race had come, but also to find out whether there was not something much greater afoot than a love affair between two young things, however strangely assorted. This it seemed to me, might bring me close to the heart of the mission on which you had sent me.

'The account I shall now give you, Sire, of the way of life of the Unites, will be woven together from my experience after long lurking among them; from study of the files in the administrative building, from listening to their rudimentary talk and watching their rudimentary emotions. I made all my observations in the one settlement where I first arrived, classified, as I soon discovered, as Life Unit 1457. My description, however, holds good for the Life Units throughout the planet as all 300,000 of them were identical in almost every particular. There were, of course, trifling differences in cultivation and raw materials and manufacture, but in all things of importance, if indeed anything was important, Unite life was uniform from pole to pole. All those delicate variations which, when I was last on Earth, still lingered on among Men and made travel on their tiny globe a constant delight, had now been abolished, stirred together into a uniform grey mass.

'I will begin by telling you of their communal existence, then describe their private lives—for private lives in a sense they may be said to have had, even though all were uniform. First of all, then, I must make you understand that the buildings in which the Unites lived, those four concrete blocks repeated in every settlement, were as much a part of their being as the shell of a lobster or crab is of the naked animal inside. Yes, whereas before individual men or families had raised walls and roof for shelter, or perhaps for ornament or ostentation, the Unites raised their buildings as a framework for the whole course of their lives; they could not escape from them, could not live away from them. In order, therefore, to describe to you the buildings, I must also describe the life cycle of a Unite from the cradle to the grave— though indeed both cradle and grave, I discovered, were private luxuries long since relinquished for the common good.

'Of the four standard tenements, the Pink Block was for the young, the Green for the cultivators, the Red for the industrial workers, and the Black Block for the administrators and the Government.

'To begin with the beginning of life, a female Unite when parturition is near leaves her married apartment or cell in the Green Block and is assigned a bed in the Labour Ward in the Pink Block. After delivery she remains there for one month feeding babies, her own and others indiscriminately, before returning to her cell and to work in the fields. Meanwhile the infant is assigned a number which will be his lifelong identification mark, will determine where he will sit, stand

and sleep, and probably also whom he will marry.

'The month-old infant is moved to Floor 0 with the rest of his age group. Soon he will learn to take it for granted that every year of his life he will move into a floor corresponding in number with his own age: that at ten years old he will be on Floor 10, at fifty on Floor 50, at sixty-five on Floor 65; what will befall him after Floor 65 he may not for some time discover. Year Groups are of the utmost importance in the Unite community, remaining always together, and every New Year either moving up one floor in the block they are occupying or, at the crucial age stages, transferring to the ground floor of the next block in the life sequence. At twenty years old the Pinks move into the Green Block; at forty the Greens move into the Red Block and at sixty the Reds go to begin their relatively short residence in the Black Block. Thus the total population of a Life Unit is always moving through its buildings like food through the intestines. Like food, too, when all value has been extracted it is spewed out at last to destruction. I do not wish to weary your consciousness, Sire, with material details about these Unites whose lives I found to be so exclusively devoted to material affairs, so little concerned with anything else, that you yourself have been severed from them. Nevertheless weariness is so just an impression to receive of Unite existence that I will not check myself from reporting a little more. As I have said, the Pinks remain in their block until the end of their twentieth year, but from twelve to sixteen they do the domestic chores of the

Life Unit, and from sixteen to twenty serve as messengers, scribes and assistants for the Black Block. At first I wondered how the young ones occupied the first dozen years of their lives, for the elementary education they were given did not advance them beyond the standard of seven-year-olds as I remember them in the past. In part the explanation must be that the young Unites were made to march and drill for hours at a stretch in the concrete yard attached to the Pink Block—exercises which I assume to have been designed to strengthen their corporate sense and weaken their individuality. Beyond this, however, the Unite metabolism was slowing down, so that all their mental functions were retarded. Their speech, as I have already suggested, had become slurred and inexpressive, and indeed, by the time they reached the Red Block, was very little used. What need was there for the play of words when all was done by rule and habit? One habit in particular had, I believe, helped to bring conversation to an end. Almost as soon as they were weaned the infants were introduced to chewing-gum, and from that time onwards were seldom without it. The adults, as I had observed on my first evening, were perfectly content to stand about in vacancy, their eyes fixed in a curious empty concentration as though the whole of their being was caught up in the rhythmic movement of their jaws.

'During their last year in the Pink Block the Unites were fitted with plastic suits and taught to fly—mass flight exercises now taking the place of drill. The suits were made in two sizes only, for an almost uniform

standard of height had been achieved with little varia-
tion even between the sexes. This world race had in
fact come very close to bodily uniformity, although I
believe slight regional peculiarities persisted in some
parts of the globe. The Unite skin colour was pale brown
with a faint greenish tinge, not at all unpleasing, and
their hair dark brown, either straight or woolly. The
usual eye colour was a dull brown and the cast of feature
blunt and lacking in definition, a kind of countenance
that went well enough with bodies thickset and service-
able. This description is applicable to the great majority,
but always a few Unites were born with blue or grey
eyes, fair hair or skin and aquiline noses. Such anomalies,
throwbacks to earlier racial types, were regarded with
so much suspicion by the community that it was custom-
ary to sterilize any individual who possessed them to any
conspicuous degree.

'Every year in every one of the 300,000 Life Units
the new twentieth Age Group marched from the Pink
Block to the Green and occupied the ground floor as
preparation for twenty years of agricultural labour. The
Greens worked two men and two women together on
smallholdings of ten acres where they raised potatoes,
oats, beans and cabbages, or their equivalents in less
temperate climates. Each allotment had a concrete hut,
as I have already described, which, in addition to tools
and seeds, housed a nanny-goat, and in due season, her
young. The few billy-goats were kept in rotation by the
allotment holders. Goat milk was given to the younger
Pinks and was made into cheese—the only good protein

in the Unite diet; the meat was wasted for there was not enough for everybody and so it could not be eaten at all. Altogether it was evident that goat-keeping was something of a survival, a vestige from a former age which no longer fitted into the economy.

'Working twelve hours a day, the Greens grew enough food to make each Life Unit self-sufficient. The food was as monotonous as that of domestic animals in the past, because meals were now taken simply to keep alive without any thought of enjoyment or any understanding that cooking could be an art. Every tenth day the Green workers, together with the whole population, had a day off, known simply as Rest Day; the old system of weeks with named days and months had been rationalized by numbering the days of the year from 1 to 365. This is not surprising, my Lord, when it is remembered that everywhere the old calendrical names commemorated the names of ancient gods.

'At the end of their year the thirty-ninth Age Group marched from the Green Block to the Red and changed their green plastic suits for red ones. After twenty years in the fields these workers had some difficulty in adjusting themselves to factory life, but its processes were now few and stereotyped, and before very long most had mastered the new mechanical movements required of them. The factories were, in any case, slow and inefficient—their products limited. The principal manufacture was of plastics: sheeting for suits, bed coverings and table tops, and paper substitute; moulded forms for lenses, domestic fittings and utensils, gramophone records and furniture. Iron was still habitually in use for agricultural implements including ploughs, but I learnt that the iron supplies of the Earth had run very low. There were some half-dozen centres on the globe where iron and cement were mined and wood grown and pulped for plastics; in these centres the Red workers undertook these labours in place of the normal factory work, making the only exceptions in the entire Unite world to the standard plan represented by Life Unit 1457. The most intricate products were simple electrical dynamos, loudspeakers and the antennae and other flight equipment. The consumption of all goods of whatsoever kind was very low, for old equipment was repaired again and again and the tenements and their furnishings were indescribably shabby.

'On completion of their fifty-ninth year, after four decades of manual toil, the Unites left the top floor of the Red Block, left the factories and moved into the low Black Block with the large chimney at the back. By this time, though still in the good health normal to Unites, they were worn out and almost without mentality, and it was in this condition that they began their career as bureaucrats and rulers. For their year on the ground-floor, it is true, their duties were slight. They were responsible for the domestic management of the tenements, but as this now proceeded almost as instinctively as that of an ant heap there was little for them to do. They had occasionally to order cement for repairs to the fabric or renew utensils; occasionally one, whose vitality was more than normal, might see himself as a

new broom and initiate a campaign for replacing broken
door-handles or missing hinges. Most of the time, however, they rested, always chewing gum, or went to
stare silently at the Pinks during their drill and flight
practice. All account keeping and the writing out of
orders was done for them by the Pink assistants, still
in the freshness of their fifteenth year. On the second
floor the Blacks supervised food production, on the third
industrial production, on the fourth the supply of raw
materials. On the fifth floor the 65th Age Group con-
stituted a government or cabinet some two hundred
strong, all of them supplied with a badge of office, con-
sisting of a ruler divided into ten equal units of measure-
ment, each of them marked with the figure 1. Their
duties were considerable: they had to control the number
of births (of which I shall have more to say presently); to
decide on sterilizations and above all to approve all the
orders issued by the first, second, third and fourth floors.
In addition, there were certain matters of general policy,
matters involving change in the ancient order of Unite
life which were regularly debated, if debate is the word
to describe their slow and rambling interchanges. Such
were the abolition of the month of natural suckling by
Unite mothers and the abolition of goats. No decisions
were ever taken, as each government was superannuated
before their deliberations had made any progress.

'I have now described to you, my Lord, the full
course of Unite communal life and it remains to tell
you of their communal death. The last act of the 65th
Age Group on the last day of the year was to approve

their own deaths. When other Groups were changing floors or tenements, they filed into a small room, known as the Finis Chamber, and were locked in by the first of the 64th Age Group now assuming government. When suffocation was complete their bodies were tipped down a shute into the furnace with the large chimney and their ashes were carried out to the fields, where their application on New Year's Day was the nearest approach to symbolic ritual in all Unite life.

'There was no doubt that this system of control and government, by the most dulled and exhausted part of the community, had originally been devised to prevent the overweening bureaucracies and tyrannies in which attempts at social justice usually ended among the human societies I had known. Indeed, this intention had perfectly succeeded, but it was my own conviction that individual government would soon have died out altogether among the Unites had not the extraordinary upheavals I shall describe happened in time to prevent it. Otherwise the Unite settlements would have reached a degree of instinctive behaviour comparable to that already achieved during many millions of years by various communal insect species—and you, my Lord, would never again have been enriched by the experiences of Man on Earth.

'I must now tell you of the private lives of the Unites, for the source, after all, of all your former delight lay in the individual man and woman. Marriage or mating took place among the Unites as soon as they moved into the Green Block, a time when the out-of-door life of agricultural labour was supposed to allow them the healthiest conditions for the begetting and bearing of children. While they were still in the Pink Block, at meals, for drill and queuing, boys and girls had been arranged alternately according to their order of birth. Although I found it was still theoretically possible for any couple within one Age Group to mate, it had become the universal custom for each young male to take the female who habitually sat or stood on his left hand side. This pairing was so simple and immediate that the couples moved straight into the married apartments provided for the entire population of the Green and Red tenements. Each woman was normally expected to bear two children and was sterilized after the second birth, but to make good deaths by accident and misadventure, a few had to be left their fertility, and might at any time be ordered to bear a third infant. This regulation, essential if the population was to remain an exact fit in its buildings, was almost the only element in life which was not by now perfectly automatic. It occupied quite half the time of the government whose members filled scores of files of plastic memoranda in their efforts to grapple with the mathematical problems involved.

'A married apartment consisted of a single room with cement walls roughly washed in the colour of the Block—Red or Green; the furniture of a plastic bed, chest, table and two chairs. The lighting was from a single pallid, fluorescent tube in the ceiling. It burned whenever the inmates were at home, for, as I noticed on my first evening, the tenements were windowless. When they woke on their plastic pallets no Unite could have any idea whether outside it was a golden day with light pouring from the sun; whether there was soft rain or an iron frost. Nor could he conceive any desire to know. What interested me most about these apartments, because it showed the survivals from the rich human past which still ran as tenuous veins in the Unite world, was the presence in each one of a picture let into the cement above the functionless rudiments of a fireplace and mantelpiece. Every apartment in every Green Block throughout the globe (I assured myself of this) had a reproduction of Van Gogh's *Cornfield*, while in the Red Blocks their place was taken by some twentieth-century abstract painting including features which resembled cog-wheels and driving-belts. These pictures were crude-ly printed on plastic sheets and had been reproduced so many times that not only were they entirely worthless as works of art but hardly to be identified with the original. In the Van Gogh, for example, where there should have been one of the most lovely singing birds, the skylark, springing above the corn, there appeared instead a diminutive Unite, stretching his plastic wings. The Black Apartments had texts instead of pictures: up to the fourth floor a highly corrupt version of the Red Flag, while on the Government floor the place was occupied by the words Dust To Dust. This at first seemed to me a too cruel reminder of the threat under which the 65th Group lived, but I soon discovered that, in so far as they were aware of the words at all, they took them to be an exhortation to keep their cells clean.

114

'It was in these small cement cells, either in darkness or under the dismal glow of the fluorescent tube, that the love life of the Unites was enacted. No wonder, my Lord, that your vision was no longer brightened by those bright sparks of human passion that once rained across it. As I have described, the manner of Unite marriage or pairing was completely impersonal; nothing endured among them of the delicately adjusted individual attraction of affinities and contrasts which in mature men and women could inspire a mutual love like a musical harmony and leave them full of tenderness and innocence. If Unite mating was decided solely by chance, their coupling was short, violent and dull, the man lying upon the passive woman and relieving his need with no more feeling than a dog. Couples continued to cohabit throughout their working life in the Green and Red Blocks, but when at sixty they reached the Black Block they parted, the men and women moving into small separate cells. It was astonishing to me to discover that after forty years of copulation, mechanical but persistent, the Unite males seemed never again to feel the slightest urge towards it once they had crossed the threshold of the Black tenement. In this they were quite unlike their predecessors, among whom old men still had desires to satisfy, as best they might, long after time had robbed them of the means. At first I thought that in this one matter the Unites were superior, but I soon saw it to be only another proof of their loss of individuality. The old *voyeurs* and users of sexual aids at least had the will to suffer and to pick up crumbs of joy. With

the Unites the habit of continence was as automatic as
the habit of indulgence. The only other comment I have
to make is that the differentiation of their sexual organs
and functions was the sole distinction between the lives
of the males and females. Otherwise the Unites enjoyed
complete sex equality.

'Apart from copulation and sleep the married apartments had few uses. Each floor throughout the Green
and Red Blocks had its shower, its lavatories and canteen.
The canteen was furnished with massive cement tables
and plastic-topped concrete benches. Along the side of
the table ran plastic-lined troughs, with depressions
opposite each place, into which thick soup, porridge
and pulses were ladled by the young Pink servitors. When
the food was eaten these troughs could readily be swilled
out with a jet of water. On the end wall of each canteen
was a picture similar to those in the cells except for its
much larger size. To my amazement I found that this
was an extremely debased but still unmistakable render-
ing of the *Last Supper* by Leonardo da Vinci. This, my
Lord, was a work by a great artist painted at a time when,
above all others, men were full of confidence in themselves and in the glory of their species. One of those ages
in their history, Sire, when human achievement made
the most brilliant of those burning arcs that illumined
your vision. The subject, too, represents in an exalted
form one of the ritual feasts by which Men strove to
reunite themselves in the unity of your Being. I imagined how the provision of this picture in each Unite
canteen had probably long ago been won as a concession

by some surviving religious body already atrophied and facing extinction.

'The workers ate in the canteens what were known as First and Third Meal; Second Meal, at midday, was eaten at work in factories and allotments. After Third Meal (summons to the canteen was by siren as I had heard my first morning) the Age Group moved into its Common Room and there sat drinking Sopo-Sola and listening to a form of music played by relayed gramophone. Sopo-Sola was the only Unite indulgence; unlike the drinks favoured by former Men, which were all stimulants to the spirits, this beverage had a slightly soporific effect. It completed what had already been done by twelve hours of toil to banish all thought and feeling from the Unite mind. Each night the music was produced by a single long-playing record; there were ten in the Unite world repertory and they were always played in the same order, a steady repetition in ten-day cycles which soothed and satisfied the audience, much as I remember the repeating of stories used to please young children in earlier times. As with the pictures the tunes were strangely distorted derivatives of pieces which had been popular of old, always with the rhythm simplified and exaggerated. Each programme ended with these chanted words: "All Unites are born equal and shall die equal. The level way of equality stretches before us for ever and ever. Work is equality and equality Work. Unites the Human Race. Amen." After which the sirens sounded again and the audience filed off to their apartments.

'It did not take me long, Sire, to learn this unvarying routine of Unite life, and I wondered, could it be possible for these creatures, still with all the parts of the Men I remembered, to endure this sorry-go-round of sleep, food, work and slackness. Had they no longer any aspiration, any need for emotional experience, adventure—rivalry even? When the Rest Day came round I discovered the answer. These urges had not quite faded, but they had hardened and narrowed into a craving for excitement; a compulsive urge with no outlet in creative forms.

'On Rest Days the whole population of the settlement formed queues at the four entrances to the great circular buildings known as the Tower, and I, my Lord, more than once penetrated with them. The atmosphere inside was oppressive. The cause of this oppression was in part physical, for the enclosing concrete walls were lofty enough to give the feeling of being closed in, at the foot of a gigantic cylinder; but in part it was due to some emotional charge in the Unites themselves, a concealed excitement. The atmosphere, in truth, was like a combination of that which used to prevail at a football match with the religious and erotic emotion present in the bull-ring. Yet at first there seemed nothing to account for such emotion. I found that the inside of the concrete shell supported a projecting flange which formed a spiral from top to bottom of the walls—not a constant slope but broken with many sudden rises and drops such as were always characteristic of switchbacks. Unites of both sexes, mostly Greens or fully grown Pinks,

were the performers, the rest of the settlement crowded
on to benches which filled three-quarters of the central
floor space of the Tower. The remaining quarter had
the appearance of a stage—a D-shaped concrete platform
dusted with sand. Performing at the Tower was voluntary, the only purely voluntary activity in the whole
course of Unite existence. Those who were going to take
part mounted to a platform at the top of the spiral where
from below they looked like midgets, so great was the
height of the wall. Here on the platform they embarked
in little open cars which ran on rails down the switch-
back flange. The cars were fitted with brakes, but the
most reckless drivers were expected to dispense with
them, hurtling round the spiral at rates which approached a hundred miles an hour on the steepest
gradients. What interested me most, my Lord, about
these cars, was that in them alone there survived something of the creative fantasy which was so often manifest
among even the simplest of Men when I was last on
Earth. They were painted in brilliant colours and were
shaped to suggest dragons, birds or grotesque human
beings; some were even embellished with fragments
of brass ornaments which were evidently of very great
age. I could see at once, my Lord, that just as the Tower
was the only place in which any emotion was generated,
so these toboggans showed the last manifestations of
that human imagination which once served you so well.
This was not the high humane imagination of the *Last
Supper* but the grotesque form that gave rise to gargoyles
and other Gothic carvings, to the totem poles, masks,

fetishes and all creations of the more primitive human races I remembered, to say nothing of the carnival figures, and the beasts of the roundabouts that perhaps came nearer than any other forms to the origin of these Unite cars.

'As the sport went on (and cars were constantly being hoisted from the bottom of the spiral to its summit) both drivers and the vast audience grew more and more excited. The drivers yelled triumphantly as they took the main plunges, while the crowd murmured, shouted, groaned, at displays of daring and timidity. Still, during my first attendance, I could not understand the increasing tension, that dark erotic undercurrent of expectant emotion. Then, with ghastly suddenness, the secret was made known. A Pink driver had just received a cheer for shooting a crest at top speed, when his car appeared to be switched from the rail, to run to the side of the flange, tip up and in so doing to catapult the Pink Unite high into the air above us. All faces turned upwards, their countless lenses flashing, and a tremendous murmur filled the whole vast concrete cylinder. The shiny pink figure was spreadeagled for a moment against the sky, fluttering his useless wings, then he hurled down and fell with a loathsome sound upon the sanded concrete stage in front of the audience—now risen to its feet—a vast swaying mob. Attendants ran forward, swathed the body in a plastic sheet and carried it away. As the audience sank back on to the benches a fearful stink of sweat rose from it, the horrid sweat of intense excitement breaking out inside thousands of plastic skins. After this climax the performers went on to finish their turns, but there seemed now to be an emotional vacuum in the Tower. We were very conscious of the rattle and roar of the plunging cars and the hollow unconvincing shouts of the drivers; the audience itself was no longer caught up and held as one body— it had disintegrated. With the kill the afternoon was over.

'When my researches had revealed to me the whole course of Unite private and social life, I could not fail, Sire, to compare it with the prognostications for the probable future of humanity current when I was last among Men. At that distant time in the past some thought the future would be brilliant, that Mankind would achieve a World Community with complete social justice and would then be able to use science to make them the masters not only of Earth but of other planets in the solar system, and also to bring them comfort, fulfilment and happiness. Others thought it would be dark and tragic, that cruel tyrannies would enslave all men, or that wars would destroy them utterly. What in fact had happened? The ideals of the few noble-minded men, who had believed all should be equal, had been achieved more completely than had seemed remotely possible. A society had been established where there was no privilege and no tyranny of any kind, where rule was by consent and all had their turn as rulers. A society, moreover, that had banished war. If the manner of their death seemed cruel, it was easy to see how that system, too, had been brought about as a necessary part of full equality. Why should one man

live longer than another? Yet in effect no future fore-
seen by erring man in the past could have been so tragic
as this harmless round of work, breeding and death.
Without privilege it seems that excellence was lost;
the ending of all conflict diminished energy; the reduc-
tion of social opposition, of difficulty, robbed life of
much of its shape, its savour. Reason had prevailed, but
without fire and imagination to fight against it, rapidly
declined into habit. Passions were diverted from warfare,
but with them into the Tower went what was left of
the creative emotions that had inspired human love,
religion and art.

'It is not difficult, my Lord, to link this account of the
generalities of Unite life with the particular events
which it was my task to follow, for it was as I left the
Tower after my first attendance there that I again came
into contact with their hidden currents. I deliberately
made my way close beside the offices at the main entrance to the Tower where the body had been taken,
and where, as I rightly guessed, the switch was worked
which controlled the car of death. Here, it seemed to
me, I might find Unites whose work set them apart
from the mass and might serve to stir their imagination.

'I was right, and indeed perhaps you were always
with me in my intuitions. In the control room I recognized the girl's lover. He and his companions had pulled
back their plastic head pieces and were wearing goat skin
caps. Goat skins, too, were hanging on the wall half
concealing the drab concrete, and above the death-lever
itself was fixed a fine pair of goat horns. I also noticed

on the opposite wall a row of miniature brass crowns, rough imitations of the great crown of the Cave and evidently made from scraps of the brass fittings from the Tower cars.

'The other Unites addressed the lover as Dante. I can hardly express to you, Sire, the pathetic incongruousness of the name of one of the greatest poets, one of your greatest servants of former times, being assumed by this young creature still only struggling back into bare humanity. Men would once have said, too, that his ardent passion was worlds apart from the poet's love for Beatrice. But for you who are the Unity of all things, there can be no such division and indeed, perhaps, you have had more delight from the sparks of human passion than from the clear glow of sacred love that is closer to your own Being. Besides, in the temporal world of these creatures, love having faded altogether from their planet, it had to be fired again in the carnal furnace before it could once more be refined.

'Two of the Tower attendants brought the body, still wrapped in plastic, into this curious sanctuary and laid it on the table before the lever. It was sadly broken, yet on the face, strangely enough, there was still that curve of the lips by which human beings formerly expressed their recognition of happiness.

'The elderly Red Unite, who worked the lever, was known as Milton; he and Dante stood at the head and foot of the corpse until Dante stepped forward and opened the plastic tunic to show a crown tattooed on his breast.

"Today the sacrifice has fallen to one of us. I pro-

123

nounce this to be Voltaire, twentieth to be enrolled
in the fellowship of the Crown-bearers. It has been
granted to him to make the supreme gesture of
voluntary death, the highest form in which for the
present we can express our recognition of the possible
glory of life. We, his fellows, who must remain a little
longer as the breathing dead, promise here, before the
wreckage of his body, to fulfil his sacrifice. Honour to
Voltaire, honour and obeisance."

All the Unites knelt and made the triple sign, touching
their breasts, where I could guess they too bore the mark
of the crown, their hearts and their foreheads.

"In the name of all Crown-bearers and of the Three
of the Cave we consign Voltaire to the earth and
declare that another crown inscribed with his one and
individual name shall be added to those of our martyrs.
Equality must be destroyed. Halleluja."

Dante finished his brief oration, and crude and slightly
ridiculous though it was, I could only be touched by the
emotion of the whole meeting and by a use of language
which was at least more expressive than the mono-
syllables and few set phrases of the Unites among whom
I had been moving. I had learnt for the first time that
my experience of the cave did not represent an isolated
pocket of atavistic emotion, but was related to a wide-
spread organization working with the ardour I had known
of old to end the dismal horrors of Unite existence.

'You will forgive me, Sire, if I show myself an eager
partisan in these Earthly affairs. During my earlier
centuries on the planet I had formed an attachment

to the human race, for these creatures who are condemned to so much suffering from their intimations of your Being. Now I saw how ideals they had faithfully believed to be noble had led them to this long decline, this Descent of Man. I could not fail to feel an attachment for those who were trying to rouse their species from their lethargy, lift it once more into the realm of your consciousness. So you will forgive me if in executing your command to learn what was happening upon Earth, I entered for a time into the cause of the Crown-bearers, shared their hopes and endeavours?'

The Being of God signified his forgiveness, but with a faint intimation of divine impatience—enough to suggest to his messenger that when he resumed his story he should try to hold in check his inclination towards a florid prolixity.

'Voltaire's body was removed for secret burial by night, all inhumation, as you will remember, having long been forbidden. About a dozen more Unites, mostly Greens with a few Pinks and Reds, who had been among the spectators in the Tower, now crowded into the little room, filling it with the smell of plastic and heat which was prevalent whenever two or three were gathered together. The ritual over, an ordinary meeting was held which gave me valuable information as to what was afoot in Life Unit 1457. Each Unite in turn opened his tunic to expose the crown, made the sign of three, touched the lever and repeated with the solemnity always characteristic of members of secret societies: "Equality must be destroyed". Then Milton spoke in the simple language which was all he could command.

' "We do well. The fellowship grows like a cabbage. We have many new recruits among the Pinks and two of them are here now. Da Vinci will speak to us. In all the Blocks there have been meetings of Crown-bearers to read and study the Books. At all meetings Dante has arranged for difficulties to be explained with the guidance of the Cave. With his help also all there learn lists of new words and verses of poetry. We know now it is no good to have members without instructing them. It was because the members were not changed that the secret societies failed in the past. They tried to continue old traditions but they grew fainter and without meaning. Now we work to open the head and heart of each one. Fellow Crown-bearers, I know the importance of what I say, for I myself have experienced change. It is only beginning. I crawl where Dante begins to fly, but already life does not look the same. I see that there could be choice and looking upwards and striving. Honour to the Three and to our Martyrs. Equality must be destroyed."

'Now one of the Pink Unites, he who was graced with the name of Da Vinci, rose to speak. He had grey eyes and a large bony nose, and he leaped up with an energy and quickness altogether exceptional among Unites. I noticed many of the Crown-bearers to be aberrants from the standard Unite type. But whether they joined a secret society because exceptional mental capacity went with these physical peculiarities, or whether they joined because these peculiarities turned society against them,

I never could determine. Whichever the cause, it appeared to me that such physically distinguished individuals were exceptionally open to the new ideas. Da Vinci himself was in any case at the most alert stage of Unite life: a nineteen-year-old Pink who was learning to fly and managing the affairs of the government, and who had not yet been dulled by the monotony of unvaried labour.

' "I bring you greetings from the Pink Block—I who am the first Pink to address a leaders' meeting. I report that the Crown-bearers having at last penetrated among us the cause spreads fast, for we of the fifteens to twenties have often felt restless and unhappy, have known without being instructed that life was not always as it is now. We had our dreams both sleeping and awake. Therefore we are able to respond to your promise of the opportunity for service, for love and thought." Then he added, with naive boastfulness: "Do not rate us low because we are young. Our work in the Black Block can give us power. Who else is it but the Pinks who have prevented decisions against goat-keeping and the suckling of infants? The Administrators and Government are our tools. When the hour of revolution comes, we can do much to speed it; we will throw out the Blacks, the moribund old dullards——"

'Dante motioned him to sit down, it may be because he felt this abuse was against the spirit of the movement, or it may be because a man so deeply in love hates all roughness. Da Vinci stopped speaking, taking the rebuke with good grace, and the second Pink Unite stepped forward and made the triple sign. To the astonishment of the meeting the open tunic revealed the breasts of a girl.

' "Crown-bearers," she cried, with a nearer approach to excitement than I had witnessed before in any of her sex. "Crown-bearers, you do wrong! Why have you forgotten the females? I know that one of the Three is a woman. I know that our Commander Dante loves her and is inspired by her. But you scorn the Unite females. At present they are sluggish; they are by nature against your hopes and desires. Yet you must win them over, the young ones, if you are to have your way. Otherwise when the day comes to act they will hold back the men from your cause. Wherever you light a flame they will stamp it out with their dull feet. I am an attendant in the Labour Ward and there, after pain and fear, the females are more likely than at any other time to listen to your message. Already since I knew Da Vinci I have done what I can among them, but you must do much more. Crown-bearers, win over the women or you will not win at all."

'Her face, my Lord, was of the heavy Unite cast, yet when she spoke some liveliness came into her eyes. In the past I had always found it hard to understand how that ball of muscle, pigment, lenses, blood vessels and other biological machinery could express so much of the spirit of a Man. Yet it was so. Even small children formerly had something in their gaze beyond what could be read in the bright eyes of animals. As they matured the quality of their expression intensified, either declining to feebleness and brutality, or rising to reveal the fire, the mystery, the suffering of the inner life. If in the past when every man, woman and child had something of humanity and their own experience showing in their eyes, I was puzzled to explain how this could be, it was no easier now to understand what had happened when a gleam of spirit suddenly informed the lifeless Unite stare. With Dante it was always brightly burning, breathed upon by his love; with this woman a gleam came with her animation only to fade again as it subsided; and often in the future I was to see its first flickering emergence in eyes which until then had never been quickened.

'At last, Sire, I left this meeting comforted by the thought that with its mixture of aspiration and courage with absurd inadequacy it was already very human. More readings and instructions were being arranged; a campaign among the women and further proselytizing among the Pinks; an effort to rouse a few more of the life-weary Reds. As I withdrew my presence, I was sure the dull surface of Unite life would soon be stirred by their strategies. It seemed evident to me that after long ages in which some traces of nonconformity, some slender tradition of opposition had persisted in the secret societies but grown ever weaker and more meaningless, there was now a vigorous current in the other direction. The forces of revolution were growing fast and would soon come into the open.

'For a considerable time, however, the Crown-bearers continued to work inconspicuously and in secret. The campaign in the Labour Ward was initiated with the help of the attendant who was herself instructed and roused, until I was able to see her no longer as a female Unite but as a woman. Those few mothers who seemed to show signs of affection for the babies they were suckling were instructed how there had been a time when all mothers kept their own children and that they themselves should be allowed to keep theirs. Then they were told simple tales from the great love stories of the past to try to convey to their minds something of the joy of individual love between a man and a woman. They were even, it must be confessed, Sire, shown pictures of the lovely clothes women formerly wore to make themselves as pretty as the birds and flowers of that happier time; many who could not respond to the idea of love and affection when described to them in words, could be reached through this appeal to the senses.

'Meetings to read and expound books brought from the Cave went on in the cells of Pink and Green Crown-bearers, and other groups met to draw and paint or to look at one another's pictures. The only pigments to be had were the standard pink, green, red and black, all of very poor quality. Very many of the artists chose to paint their visions of the Three and seemed naturally to adopt the stiff, Byzantine style formerly often found in the art of children; there they were in picture after picture these three heads, the delicate face, the bearded face and the heavy dark face, hieratical and poetic.

'All these solemn gatherings held in the cramped

cells made me think of the educational classes attended by working people during the last century or so of my previous visit; there was, however, one great difference; whereas then the workers were studying because they had a long-frustrated desire for education, because they thought they ought, or to improve their economic position, the Unites approached books and paintings as an unknown territory, one which proved inaccessible to some of them, a slow but profoundly stirring relevation to others.

'When the patient work of preparing their living material was felt by Dante and the other leaders to have gone on long enough—by which time many of their followers had not only given up chewing gum, my Lord, but even had something of humanity sitting in their eyes—when it had gone on long enough they advanced from these private activities to stage tentative demonstrations in public.

'The first of these which I witnessed took place in the canteen on the tenth storey of the Green Block, the storey known as Floor 30 and occupied by the corresponding Age Group. When the thirty-year-olds had shuffled in and were waiting for the Pinks to ladle out to them some of the mush served for Third Meal, one of them stood up in his place immediately below the *Last Supper* and pronounced a once familiar Latin grace. Although his pronunciation came hardly nearer to the original than the reproduction to Leonardo's painting, unlike the picture it was expressed with great seriousness and feeling.

'I watched eagerly for the reaction. There was none. A few of the Unites sitting closest to the speaker turned and stared at him with expressions perhaps more vacant than was normal, but all the rest picked up their worn old plastic spoons and began to sup from the trough. In my exasperation with their apathy, I wondered whether they would have shown any interest if all the species of birds and beasts which they had exterminated from their planet had suddenly wriggled, walked, flown into the canteen.

'At that moment I saw most clearly how the difficulty of revolution did not now lie in overthrowing a dangerous power but in rousing the Unites, sunk in centuries of well-ordered vacancy, to any action, even to any emotion. Without injustice as much as they were without desire, what was there to provoke them to struggle? More surely than ever before I was made to understand the importance in the human world as I had known it of opposition and contrast. Their spinning planet confronted men with mountain and plain, land and water, night and day; nature had shaped them male and female; similarly in their lives they had need of the possibilities of suffering and joy, of justice and injustice, of discipline and rebelliousness; to be able to rise and free to fall. All these opposites, Sire, which challenged them to delight and serve you so well, the opposites which through them were made whole in the unity of your Being.

'Dante and his friends persisted in their demonstrations, but though I believe they brought in some new recruits to the Crown-bearers they still made as slight an impression on society at large as a mosquito probing an elephant's back or meteorites bombarding the Earth. In the entrance halls of the Green and Red Blocks I noticed one day that crowns had taken the place of the stencilled cabbage and cog-wheel, while brass crowns from the Tower appeared on the heads of the central figure of Equality in all the Blocks. Youngsters in the Pink Block began to play games in the drill ground and their elders, flying over the Square in their practice flights, dropped plastic leaflets inscribed "EQUALITY MUST BE DESTROYED"; copies of the same notice were posted over the inscription "Dust to Dust" in the rooms of the Government.

'Most daring of all the Crown-bearers won access to the rough and ready sound-relay system. On more than one evening the musical record was interrupted by a voice, which I recognized as Dante's, reading simple romantic and heroic stories (with a moral comparing their ideals with those of Unite society), and even inviting listeners to attend meetings.

'All these gallant efforts were silently swallowed in the morass of Unite life—life in which time seemed to have lost all significance, being almost without change or direction. There was nothing but the inevitable ageing of the individual organisms and their passage through the tenements from Labour Ward to Finis Chamber.

'I determined, my Lord, before returning to the Cave which attracted me so powerfully, I would thoroughly sink myself in this morass, so that instead of noting facts like a foreign anthropologist I should myself experience its quality, know the everydays of Life Unit 1457. Day after day I abandoned myself to the routine from the first dull wakening and switching on of the electric light and the siren wailing for First Meal to the weary aerial procession back from work, and the drowsy evenings when one sat stupefied with Sopo-Sola and flooded to every corner of the mind with the mechanical music of the loudspeakers.

'The strong pervading physical impressions were of perpetual crowds in and round the tenements and factories and monotonous labour in the small holdings— all to the accompaniment of steadily moving jaws, teeth slithering on gum. With this went the wretched, insistent shoddiness of plastic and concrete, the lack of any grace or of any single object that showed the mark of having been shaped by an individual hand or conceived in an individual imagination.

'The pervading spiritual impression, Sire, was of utter passivity. The Unites were deeply conditioned to the idea that once they were born all their lives must run along identical and immovable lines; they had long since surrendered all possibility of creation, of opposition, or peculiarity. One symptom of their condition, physical and spiritual together, which I found most melancholy in contrast with what I had known before, was that with the grim exception of the Tower and what went on there, everything in the Unite world was for practical use. The buildings were mere containers for basic forms of bodily existence; clothes, utensils, furni-

ture, food, served their low and hopeless purpose—
nothing more. Greetings and other agreeable formalities
of word and gesture had been forgotten equally with
all more exalted rituals and symbolism; they had vanished with religious observances and with named days,
weeks, months and festivals, all the things which had
given shape and colour to the human year. Language,
the words which Men once used so magically to express
and heighten their intuitions had, as I have already
shown, been reduced to the bare rudiments of necessary
communication. There were, it is true, the absurd
reproductions of paintings and the concrete figures and
reliefs in the tenements, but nobody any longer really
saw them and it was doubtful whether they would ever
be replaced. The canned music and Sopa-Sola may, I
consider, be recognized as necessities, for without them
the Unites would surely have died of boredom and
inanition.

'Perhaps it was this utilitarianism more than anything
else which made Unite existence fall so far below even
the worst of human life in former days. Peasants of old
had lived from birth to death almost as helplessly, with
almost as little hope of escape, but their life's course
had been decked with fantasy and symbol, with simple
art and ritual, with very many things that were of no
use in daily life except to make it human and significant.
Now utilitarianism itself was at its most base, for needs
and expectations had been so much reduced that all
were perfectly satisfied. To have no desire is far more
dreadful than for desire to remain unfulfilled.

'When at last I felt I had touched the depths of
experience in this society I was free to seek out the Cave
and to learn more of its troglodytes. You will understand,
Sire, the great longing I felt to retreat there after my
self-imposed exposure to physical and spiritual poverty. In
that secret rock fastness with its glitter and darkness and
rich or curious furnishings, I would be not only in the very
heart of the revolutionary movement, but also in the one
place where something of ancient holiness survived, where
I could meet again with that abundantly endowed humanity I had once loved.

'I will first tell you the history of the Three, making a
single narrative from the fragmentary information of their
most extraordinary story which I was able gradually to ac-
cumulate.

'I learned that when, as I shall later describe, Men using
atomic power had levelled much of the surface of the
planet in order to have more space for food-growing and
habitation, they had left a considerable mountain mass in
a region which I guessed to be that of the European Alps. (I
have told you, my Lord, how these Alps had represented
some of the loftiest, because the most recently formed, of
the odd rucking of the Earth's surface which had taken
place long before humanity had been brought into being.)

'The surviving mountain mass, of great height but no
large extent, had been assumed to be uninhabited, but in
fact there was a village in a little valley completely enclosed
by peaks and ridges. It had been founded by refugees
from all the royal and noble houses of Europe, together
with a few American millionaires from the Riviera, at the

time when the third and most violent revolution established perfect justice and equality and set the human race surely on the way to Unitehood. The refugees had found cattle and sheep feeding among the flowery Alps, abandoned by their peasant owners after some holocaust, and they themselves had contrived to bring an amazing collection of regalia, jewellery and gold coins and also (for there were always a few educated men and women among the European aristocracy) books representing most of the greatest literature since the sixteenth century. This community where no one was of less than noble rank —the millionaires had rapidly secured their promotion— managed to maintain themselves through great stretches of time while out in the world around them Men were very gradually but inevitably turning into Unites. It had from the first established a court where the senior monarch among the refugees and his descendants became the recognized Royal Family. Court ceremony was, indeed, of quite unusual intricacy, for to please so cosmopolitan a group of crowned heads and nobility some item of ritual was adopted from each one of their kingdoms and principalities. In the humble chalet which was the palace it was impossible to move about in a normal fashion for everyone was on his or her knees, walking backwards, bowing, curtseying, kissing hands or toes from dawn to dark. Christenings, betrothals, marriages and funerals were also celebrated with all possible pomp and circumstance. The little kingdom, though prosperously self-supporting and as full of treasure as Aladdin's cave, demanded hard work from its subjects, and in truth everyone except the Royal Family itself had to do some manual labour. This caused no difficulties, however, for by appointing themselves Blue Stick-in-Waiting to the Pigsties, Scythe-Bearer to His Majesty, Count of the Privy, Lady-in-Milking to the Herd and so forth, they were well satisfied and found that they enjoyed their jobs quite as well as their aristocratic duties of fighting, killing animals and gardening. Love affairs went on much as before and, it seems, deteriorated only a little in the quality of their experience.

'If, Sire, it must have been reminiscent of the type of performance once known as comic opera this social system worked very well; every individual had a place in an organic society and considered it to be honourable; there was reasonable opportunity for families to move up and down the hierarchy according to the ability, industry or astuteness of their members. Though in the whole of its immensely long history the kingdom appears to have produced no individuals of high genius—and indeed, as we know, its life produced virtually nothing that entered into your experience—it always maintained a court scholar and schoolmaster who was often able and industrious. A long line of such scholars had not only puzzled out the history of Man up to the time of the last refugee's arrival in the valley, but had also kept sound chronicles for their own kingdom. Of Unite evolution they knew nothing, for on the only occasion when two daring young men left the valley to explore the plains they were never heard of again. Yet on the whole it can be said that in the peace and calm of their refuge this people achieved a high tradition for learning, philosophy and true wisdom.

'For many thousands of years the simple affairs of the kingdom were peaceably managed and there was no more unrest than that caused by the ceaseless dynastic plotting of the women seeking to make the best marriages for their own children, always with the hope that in a generation or two their descendants would wed into the Royal Family. There had been a few instances of treason and of pretenders to the throne, but none had gone far enough seriously to divide the community before they were settled by execution, assassination or negotiation.

'Then at last the Kingdom betrayed itself through the evil aspect of its virtues. By ill fortune a number of Unites, desperate from hunger after their crops had failed, came upon the valley while searching for new land. Alarmed by the sight of beings comparable to themselves and yet so evidently alien, these Unites armed themselves with stones, flew over the village hurling their missiles at the inhabitants. However the people of the valley had developed archery partly as a sport, partly, in the absence of gunpowder, to maintain the traditions of a warrior aristocracy. They shot at the flying Unites and pierced their gas sacs so that they came either planing or tumbling down into the valley bottom where they were taken prisoner.

'All that was worst in this hierarchical society now came to the surface. Against the passionately expressed counsel of the reigning court scholar—who was in fact the Sage of the Cave—the Unites were held in the valley and used as slaves. Immediately half the king's subjects remembered their noble origins and refused to do any more demeaning work, Unites were bought and sold for large expenditures of treasure and before long a few families owned them all. The king tried to make their owners work and so restore the old social harmony and justice, but they resisted, armed their slaves and launched a civil war. So in a few weeks this venerable social pyramid toppled in ruins. Inevitably, to restore order, the strong man of the rebels, the late Count of the Privy, set up a tyranny over the sadly reduced population, and found it necessary to exterminate the Royal Family and most of the immediate household. The Sage, whose wisdom had been so tragically proved, managed to escape together with Rachel, the king's youngest daughter who had been his favourite pupil. They carried with them about a score of the Sage's books, the crown and cup habitually used in coronations and the other relics I had seen in the Cave. They also contrived to drive off two milking ewes and a young ram.

'The account I can give of their journey, Sire, is very incomplete for neither the Princess Rachel nor the old man was inclined to talk of their experiences. They seem to have fled down the mountains and then to have walked from Life Unite to Life Unit, hardly knowing what they hoped to do. It was then that the Sage realized for the first time that the Unites who had come to the valley were not rare freaks, but the inheritors of the whole Earth. It must indeed have been a dreadful discovery for a man who had spent a happy life absorbing the finest products of human literature and philosophy, imagining them to be average samples of the genius of his race; and who had, moreover, believed that other such masterpieces were still being written by human beings by now fully recovered from past revolutions and advancing along the way to perfection. His travels soon taught him the extraordinary truth that the valley kingdom he had just seen destroying itself was all that had survived of civilization as he had understood it; a minute island in the vast grey sea of the Unite Way of Life.

'At first he must have despaired; at the Life Units there was no one to whom a traveller could appeal for help either as an individual or an official. All he and Rachel could do was to try to camp on an allotment and to barter ewe milk for vegetables; as often as not they were driven off by the Green Unites and pursued with cabbage stalks and stones. What hope of any kind was there? However, by good fortune before the Sage had made up his mind to kill himself and his companion they camped on the holding of a member of the secret society of the Crown-bearers, gaining his sympathy and all that he had of understanding. When he learnt of the existence of this society the Sage took heart; might it not after all be possible to save the Unites and swing them back on to the road of the old humanity? On being told that there was a Crown-bearer in Life Unit 1457 of such extraordinary gifts that his fame had spread throughout the society, he at once determined to seek him out.

'The journey was now made easy, for members of the society took care of the travellers in each Life Unit they had to traverse, until at last they reached 1457 and were receiving the homage of Dante in the Cave below the Rock. Dante, my Lord, was evidently an extreme case of atavism, for even before the coming of this new inspira-

tion he was more like a man of the ancient world than a
Unite. Until his meeting with true humans he had been
baffled, full of obscure dissatisfactions and urges that he
could not understand; as soon as he met them, he had
felt the power of the Sage's mind and fallen in love with
Rachel, his intuitions were explained and his gifts came
rapidly to flower.

'Until now, Sire, I have said nothing of the negro who
was to play an obscure yet profoundly important part in
the salvation of the Unites. Indeed, no one will ever know
anything of his origins and early history; presumably
there must have been a survival of unmixed native blood
in some remote part of Africa comparable to that of the
European in the valley. I can only tell you, Sire, how he
came to be one of the Three.

'The Sage and the Princess were making their way
along the edge of a lake in the dusk of a summer evening
when they heard a soft, leisurely splashing in the water and
in the half darkness could see its smooth surface broken by
an extending line of ripples. Presently the African stepped
ashore some little way in front of them. They went on
without faltering, and the Sage gave him a greeting as
they passed, whereupon the negro joined them walking
quietly at their side. I heard Rachel describe her own
sharp memory of the moment, how she became aware of
his huge figure moving close beside her, moving without
a sound, whereas their own shoes rattled on the pebbles.
She noticed the last light of the sky condensed to a glitter
in the drops of water still clinging to his skin while the
odour of the wet furs he was wearing filled her nose.

'At that time they had no word in common, for where-ever he and his people had been lurking they had kept their own tongue as well as their pure race. Even when I arrived on Earth, something like a year later, he still spoke very little—but then words were not his medium of expression.

'Well, my Lord, as I have said, the time came when I felt free to transfer my presence to the Cave and so one evening I followed Dante on his habitual visit there. As I passed the rock and dropped to the grassy hollow, I saw with pleasure that the ewes had lambed since my first visit, and also that Rachel had induced some of the wild flowers to grow round the Cave entry. As I passed the leather curtain I heard a sound which at first I thought must be an echo from the bleating of the lambs outside. It was in truth the crying of a small human infant. I had entered the fissure with the thought of at last being able to refresh myself with human wisdom and spirituality, and for a moment this thin, pale, touchingly animal cry coming from the craggy gloom within filled me with disgust and even contempt. I had thought so much of the love of Dante and Rachel, but in fact they had copulated like all members of their species and had been rewarded with the common fruit of copulation. Here was the ordinary little body oozing or secreting through seven orifices and sucking through one of them. Yet as I brought my presence into the cavern itself I was overwhelmed with shame at my lack of understanding. The girl was sitting at the foot of the couch with the crown hanging immediately behind her head, and as the light from the lamps reflected in the gold it seemed to me like one of those rayed haloes with which Christian artists used to distinguish holy men and women. It was, indeed, my Lord, the mark they chose to prove contact with your being.

'The infant was on his mother's arm and at that moment had ceased the wailing which had followed the interreption of its sucking. He and she now stared down at the father kneeling at their feet. On the instant I recognized not only an exquisite manifestation of the fusion of body and spirit in Man, but also how here in the warmth of flesh and bone another eternal symbol had been added to the Cave.

'I dwelt for some time in this place, learning the facts about the history of the troglodytes which I have already related to you, and studying their mode of life—which was regular and harmonious beyond anything I remember among Men.

'The Sage, I found, was engaged every morning in writing a history of the Decline of Mankind, much of which, between the foundation of the kingdom and his own flight from the valley, was bound to be speculative. Occasionally he consulted Dante, seeking for such rudiments of the past as might survive among the Unites, especially in the secret societies. The old man always gave some part of the day to meditation, and by way of a practical duty undertook the care of the little flock of sheep— much of whose fodder I discovered was brought by Dante from the allotments of Crown-bearers. Then every night, after Dante's arrival, he and the Sage had most earnest discussion about their work among the Unites and their plans for revolution. The young man was often discouraged by the meagre results of their educational campaign, the slow response to their demonstrations and the weary degradation of his everyday life. I noticed how, as soon as he came in, he skinned off his plastic suit with extreme disgust and dressed himself in a woollen tunic which Rachel had made for him.

'The Princess, indeed, gave much of her time to spinning and weaving, often sitting just outside the fissure while her baby lay near her. As he grew older and more active she tethered him on a woollen rein much as the sheep were tethered. She had musical gifts that were simple but true and she composed a number of songs, some lullabies, some to accompany infant games. She also had cheesemaking ditties—for this was her other most exacting task. Dante wrote them all down and had them taught to the Unite mothers in the Labour Ward and I do not doubt, Sire, that they will long be sung on Earth.

'Often when she sang inside the Cave, the African would accompany her on a drum he had most ingeniously constructed out of sheepskin and the wooden box which had held the royal crown. His own life was secret, low-pitched and without will. Indeed, it sometimes seemed to me that just as his body often lost itself in the shadows of the Cave, so his consciousness was still hardly sharply enough differentiated to belong to the world of light. When Dante was not there he liked to play with the infant or to rock it in the fleecy hammock he had made for him from the pelt of a still-born lamb. The child never showed him particular affection, yet was always quiet and good in his company.

'About sunset, during the hour before Dante came, the negro might withdraw into the innermost parts of the Cave to sing and beat the drum in most intricate rhythms, working himself up to a passionate climax when the whole cavern seemed to pulsate and its crystals, jewels and gold to form a precious encrustation on the rough fabric of sound.

'One Rest Day Dante was very late; the African had been drumming longer and more ardently than usual and Rachel was anxious for her lover, so that the atmosphere was already tense when Dante came quickly in, high-charged with excitement. He paused to make his usual formal salute of homage to the Three, but then without waiting to strip himself of his hateful Unite dress, he sat beside the Sage at the table.

' "Master," he said, "today another Crown-bearer was the sacrifice at the Tower. Afterwards at the meeting in the Lever Room, Leonardo and many of our leaders declared that the time has come to take action. Our movement has spread so fast in the Pink Block that they are straining to try themselves. The very children are infected; they play games and in their drill they fall into the form of the crown for their last exercise. If this revolutionary spirit grows even the Government will at last get wind of it, and although the Pinks scoff, saying they *are* the Government, the Blacks might make a stubborn opposition. Listening to our speakers, I was convinced, and suddenly it seemed absolutely clear to me that we must act at the end of the year, Progress Day. On that day, 365, nobody works, all the inhabitants are scattered in their cells and at a certain hour even the most sluggish Unites feel uprooted as they move from one floor to another or into a new Block. The old Government is out of the way and the new has hardly taken up its futile rulers of office. Finally, Master, and here I understand myself only dimly, this is the last year when this boy will be an infant, when he can appear before the people on his mother's arm. This is my own faith and conviction, but yours is the word of decision. Is it Yes or is it No?"

'As Dante finished speaking, I found myself rejoicing at the growth of his nature which had taken place while I had been on Earth. Now he was eloquent, authoritative, naive only with the naivety of a good man. So much had been done for him on the one hand by his share in the life of the Cave, on the other by responsibility, struggle against obstacles, the necessity of giving confidence. He was in himself a total vindication of human life as I had known it with all its evil and failure, a total condemnation of the Unite order.

'You will know, Sire, that the Sage's reply to Dante could only be Yes. He had been waiting for the Crown-bearers to feel themselves to be ready, to have built up their energy by opposing it to resistance, and now was overjoyed to let them try their strength. He was after all an old man, and a mortal man; though he might perceive and accept his position as an eternal symbol, he knew that he must die and longed with all the heart of youth to be allowed time to pass on some of the accumulated wisdom, the rare treasure of knowledge that had been entrusted to him during his life in the valley kingdom.

L*

'I will now finish my report to you, my Lord, by repeating a few speeches, recalling certain scenes, for I believe it is in this fashion, disjointed but a little detailed and particular that I can best convey the end of my third mission to the Earth.

'The day I have just described when Dante brought his tidings to the Cave was 350 in the lifeless Unite calendar; on the next Rest Day, 360, Dante read an address to the usual meeting of leaders in the Lever Room; it was stiffly worded, half proclamation, half directive.

' "On 365, Progress Day, all initiated Crown-bearers must begin to fulfil our oath to overthrow the hated tyranny of Equality. The revolution is to be launched at nine hours, the moment when, according to the inhuman rule of Unite society, every inhabitant of every Life Unit on Earth must move his habitation and when every Government has been consigned to suffocation. We shall take over the entire Black Block, including the broadcast system. A Crown-bearer will be appointed as warden to each floor in all the Blocks and they will order everyone to remain in his cell. The revolution will then be announced and the new citizens ordered to come here to the Tower where the son born to the Princess Rachel shall be hailed as our King, after which the Sage, the African, myself as Commander and all of you as recognized leaders shall swear allegiance to him and to his mother. We do not anticipate resistance, but on 365 all Pink Crown-bearers must carry Indian clubs, all Greens sharpened hoes and all Reds spanners, chisels or hammers. Special precautions must regretfully be taken in the Red Block where our member-

148

ship is weakest. There two wardens will be appointed for each floor and they will carry arms for the duration of 365.

' "All work in fields and factories will be suspended for seven days, the longest period our economy can at present allow. During that time a beginning must be made in the conversion of Unites once more into Men. Among the first measures will be one to turn cells and nursery wards into apartments and to give the babies and young children to couples fit to adopt them. Also to abolish all classification by numbers, age-groups and colour, making individuals choose their own names and restoring the old calendar. The Princess will go among them teaching cooking, and other domestic skills and filling them with her spirit; the African will teach them the arts of love, of music and dancing; the Sage will teach them from our great books.

' "I also announce that to prepare, instruct and inspire us for the revolution, on the night of 364 there will be a gathering of all Crown-bearers here in the Tower where for the first time you will be able to look on the faces of the Three. The Sage will speak to us of what has happened and what we must do. Many Crown-bearers are coming from other Life Units and from that night we may expect our revolution slowly to spread about the Earth.

' "For the last time let us salute the lever of death and our martyrs of the Tower. They had to choose the hazard of death; we hope to be free to choose the hazard of life. Equality must be destroyed! Halleluja!"

'I confess, my Lord, that I was disappointed by the awkward formality of most of this pronouncement—how much I preferred the Dante of the Cave—but then, as I reflected, many of those present were still only beginners in humanity and had little understanding of words and feelings. I was also disquieted by the mention of weapons —would hoes, clubs and hammers lead back to guns and bombs? Must the best and the worst always flourish together among Men? I fear it may be so, dear Lord, and yet I hope that at least in this one thing of destroying mortal bodies it will be otherwise. This was what was in my mind and this the direction of my prayers as I watched these beings file out, making their last obeisance to the symbol of voluntary death. Poor, pathetic figures, still dressed in their vile plastic skins, and still, O God, not only remote from the realms of your consciousness but many of them far from having recovered the stature of the humblest Men.

'It was not dark on the night of 364 for there was a clear sky of stars and a bright moon. I was waiting on the wide concrete expanse of the Yard where two hours ago the gates of the tenements had yet again snapped meanly to behind the last of the mass of returning workers. By now all those prisoners of the huge concrete shells must have been inert in their common rooms drugged with Sopo-Sola and Music Record No. 5, yet vaguely aware that tomorrow was not like all other days, as it would bring neither work nor the Tower. In particular, I imagined, the 19-, 39-, 59- and 65-year-olds were alive to something like apprehension concerning the changes (all of them for the worse) that they supposed to lie in wait for them.

'All Unites should have been inside the tenements,

150

safely behind the heavy doors, yet now as I waited near
the Tower I saw figure after figure fly overhead and
alight beside the entrance; a few of the boldest mounted
higher and higher until they were clear of the top of the
huge cylinder and could circle down within. The Pinks
had evidently been lurking in the Black Block whose doors
were not fastened at night for the reason that its inmates
never thought of going out of doors; the Greens flew in
from the convenient shelter of their allotment tool-sheds,
and the few Reds had found somewhere to hide near their
factories. Then, among those Unites descending from
above into the Tower, I noticed some who had flown in
high and from far off—Crown-bearers from other and
unknown Life Units.

'I do not know, Sire, whether I can convey to your
Omniscience how this scene rather than another could be
described as profoundly strange. In the moonlight the
huge zig-zags on the Tower walls had lost their garishness
and revealed a grotesque, barbaric force; although they,
and indeed the whole landscape, were reduced almost to
monochrome I could just distinguish the different colours
of the flyers as the shiny surface of their suits caught the
moonbeams. Sometimes, as they went past, their gesti-
culating shadows swept in an arc across the curving walls
of the Tower and it was more than ever hard to believe
that these were creatures of warm blood, guided by a
conscious purpose—indeed, by an idea.

'When I was about to leave my watching because the
last of the flyers appeared to have arrived, my line of
vision dropped to the ground and came to rest on a small

group approaching from the direction of the Cave. Milton and Leonardo were leading the way carrying the great crown slung on its woollen cords between them. The Sage came next, walking lost in thought; Rachel had one arm through his, and on her other side went Dante, carrying their son and wearing the jewelled sword. The African had dropped a few steps behind, and I had an inkling that he was alert for danger. They were just passing the corner of the Black Block, when to my helpless anguish I saw a large black object fall from the coping towards them. I thought in that instant of the pathetic delicacy of the human body with its fragile bones and yielding flesh; I even had time to picture the paper-thin skull of the infant. But there was no horror; no physical tragedy. The thing fell just behind the negro as though the assassin had failed to allow for the movement of his target. It struck the concrete with a crash, broke it and lay half buried among the fragments; it was a large, rusty iron cog-wheel.

'Inside the Tower the platform where through the centuries so many Unites had been shattered, had been prepared as a rostrum and its lunate form was outlined with candles. Three seats had been brought out from the Lever Room and hidden below goatskins and in front of them one of the most fantastic of the Tower cars had been placed to serve as a rostrum. Milton and his fellows had worked well, and now, just before midnight, nature (as Men formerly distinguished it) was surpassing them. It so happened that the moon was in such a position in the sky that it flooded that part of the Tower floor occupied by the platform, its light lying pale yet strong over the little golden tongues of the candles. The rest of the floor where the audience of Crown-bearers was gathered was blackened by the heavy shadow of the Tower wall; thus while the Three looked straight up at the dazzling disc of the moon, the audience could see only the dark blue diorama of the starry sky.

'As the Sage climbed into the car and prepared to speak, I observed to my delight how a simple smile of amusement lightened his face as he saw that his pulpit was formed from the arched necks and heads of two weird birds—remote descendants, perhaps, of the phoenix. I prepared to listen with a new light-heartedness.

' "Friends and Crown-bearers, I greet you for the first time, but have long been working for you. At last, tonight, we have come to our Revolution eve. Tomorrow we are pledged to an action which should begin the salvation of all Mankind. For long you have pronounced an oath, 'Equality must be destroyed'; tomorrow you must strike the first blow to break up its dreary, tyrannous expanse. All those among you who are still young have a great longing, that I know, to have that opportunity which all men should have to serve and be served. To feel responsibility for those below, to devote oneself to those above. That should be Man's inalienable gift, one of the gifts distinguishing him from beasts and insects. As for those who are at the summit of human society, their privileges come from those below them and all that they can achieve belongs to them. They know, too, that those great men who have been put at the head of society are as grains of dust at the foot of the colossal mystery of this universe. Look, my friends, through the depths of the starry sky above you and take it as a symbol of the mystery that dwarfs us all.

' "How is it that Men have fallen into this hopeless servitude to a social machine? How have they become Unites, creatures who seem already to be evolving into a different and lower species—and who will certainly do so if we do not check their course? I have toiled to find the answer. I have learned by heart the few great books that have survived from the past and the histories compiled in the kingdom from which I come. I have studied the present-day life of the Unites. I have attempted then to join the two, to speculate what happened after the end of the old histories and before the Unite present (for it is a small part of the degradation of the Unites that they have kept no history).

' "The story in so far as I have understood it is a tragic one, all the more wretched because during the unfolding of it the participants have become incapable of tragedy; have sunk below its level. Long ago Men, your distant ancestors, were humble in their belief in a presiding God. Knowing how very helpless they were on this planet where they had to face dangers of every kind, the death of their puny bodies from disease, starvation, savage animals, flood, earthquake and many other causes, they expressed this knowledge as the fear of God. They also expressed their understanding of the great mystery of which I have spoken as the love and honour and worship of God.

' "Then came a time of ruthlessness and brilliance.

Men sharpened the intellects seated in their brains and made of them truly marvellous instruments. Yet marvellous though they were, when turned against the heart of the mystery it was as though Men sought to reach the centre of this planet with a pin. The human intellect discovered, however, that it could attack one aspect of the mystery with great effect. It could discover the structure of matter by breaking it down into smaller and smaller parts.

' "For a time the sharpening of the mind filled Men with pride in themselves; they feared so much less, understood so much more, and ignored the heart of the mystery which was as far beyond them as ever. They saw no need to keep a God in being. There was reason for human pride, for in that age our ancestors created many of the finest products of art and thought in their history.

' "But their intellectual obsession with matter, their wish to believe that in analysing it they were solving the mystery, led them to a more and more helpless dependence upon matter; they devoted their lives, brief as your own, to grabbing and shaping matter for human use and abuse. There was, in so far as I can understand the facts, a corresponding increase in human bodies—a vast multiplication of the numbers of our species. Nearly all these vast numbers of men and women wished to own as much matter as diversely shaped as possible.

' "To satisfy this perverted hunger, our species turned to pillage the Earth with a voraciousness and lack of foresight which seem almost to imply a lack of belief in the reality of the future and of their own descendants. Soil and its vegetation, living creatures, rocks and every kind of mineral were all devoured, sacrificed to Man's obsession with matter. This was the time when much of the wild life, animal and vegetable, which had come with Man out of the remote past, was made extinct.

' "Strangest of all, in their passion for material goods, our ancestors appear to have forgotten their first material need—that of food. People after people built factories and produced factory workers so that they should have more possessions, yet did not seem to understand what was happening when it was found that no one any longer had enough of meat and cheese and butter and many other needful and delicious foods of which you yourselves have never heard but which once were abundant. They blamed their governments, not realizing that the food supplies of the Earth were running low, devoured by the industrial masses.

' "Famine, so I believe, came suddenly. Millions starved to death; whole families died among the expensive welter of their material possessions. Millions more were slaughtered in the wars that inevitably followed—wars, Crown-bearers, being the struggle of groups of Men to kill or make helpless groups of other Men. The rest left the cities where the famine had struck and devoted all the forces still left to them, the control over matter which they had won so hard, to a mighty work of levelling mountains, vivifying deserts, so that they might grow more food. It was a wonderful achievement. Natural beauty was destroyed, but Man survived. Last of all they turned to clear away the ruins of their own cities where now the scenes of horror had been mercifully obliterated by time. I found a description of one of them, a city called New York which was, perhaps, the strangest spectacle of them all. This city was built on a rocky island and its people, who beyond all others were obsessed with matter, and powerful in its control, had raised buildings so tall that your own huge tenements would not reach a quarter of the way up their precipitous sides. They were strong and well founded on rock. When Men at last returned to them, the streets, once crowded with machines and rich displays of material goods of every kind, had the appearance of gaunt and wild ravines. Their floors were covered with grass and weeds and a few of the hardiest of the flowers the late citizens had cultivated; all the millions of window-ledges, too, were trailing with weeds, and on them nested vast numbers of pigeons and jackdaws. Swifts and hawks had taken possession of the tallest towers and rats were everywhere. At dawn and sunset, the chronicler records, these ravines assumed a great beauty, but it was the beauty of Nature rather than of Man. How strange that one of the last haunts of wildness should have been created by human hands.

' "I must ask for your patience, Crown-bearers, but now I come to a part of this history which you will see is closer to the roots of Equality and the Unites. When our ancestors believed in a personal God and in their own souls, they felt that a life was justified if it prepared a fair soul for God's keeping. They also allowed that whatever the injustices of Earth, all Men were equal in the sight of God. Already, many good men taught that there should be justice also on Earth, less difference between rich and poor, the powerful and the weak, but few felt the need to listen.

' "You will understand how when our ancestors not only had destroyed God and their own souls, but had come to believe far more in the importance of matter and less in the spiritual interest of Man, it appeared to be intolerable that matter should be so unevenly distributed between man and man. The more generous the thinker, the more determined to cling to morality in spite of the loss of God, the more earnestly he fought for material equality. And now most men were ready to be inflamed.

' "Yes, they strove hard for this, and while the struggle lasted it was a noble one, for all struggle against opposition for an ideal is ennobling. But they were blind not to see that Equality was not an aim which if achieved would be good in itself; it had no virtue and no purpose except as an ideal encouraging sacrifice. This then, was the great tragedy, that it was the best, the most idealistic element in Man that set him on the long slope of slow decline.

' "At first there was another tragedy. That the generous-hearted reformers were joined in the cry for Equality by men full of the lust for power, who wanted the swarming numbers of human beings now living on Earth to be ground into uniformity so that they might control them in enormous, impersonal and terribly powerful masses. They proved the stronger, and the revolutions, the fearful bloodshed and suffering brought about in the name of Equality, led to the establishment of the most grinding tyrannies the Earth at that time had ever known. Then the good men who saw their ideal shattered were cast down, but still did not doubt that the ideal would bring happiness if only it could be attained.

' "It must, so far as I have been able to discover from records which now become tenuous, have been at about this moment of disillusion that famine struck Mankind with the horrible result I have described, so that the creed of egalitarianism came together with the near exhaustion of raw materials, the flight from the towns and the tottering fall of industrial organization. By now those who lusted after power were weakened and the more idealistic reformers could take control; on the other hand I do not doubt that there had been such damage done to culture, such an impoverishment of education, that even the best were no longer of such fine quality as before. They were, however, determined to avoid all the mistakes that had perverted earlier revolutions. So they hit upon the plan of society based upon small self-contained units, and smallholdings. They also introduced rule by all the elders so that every individual might have his turn of mild authority, and put into practice the idea of sex equality on a masculine footing which had long been a necessary part of their creed.

' "This time the revolution succeeded completely and it has endured until this hour. All men had equality of possession and of power, and in that sense perfect justice. The tendency of our species to violence and greed having been defeated, our tendency to laziness and to mental and spiritual sloth was unopposed; the species was very weary and sank fast.

' "At first material life in the small communities was tolerably comfortable and their members existed in a kind of base contentment, ready enough to be free of struggle and desire. Gradually even material standards declined. Many raw materials were exhausted, and there was less and less transport between different parts of the Earth, for apart from the difficulties of organization it threatened the perfect equilibrium of the small communities—which now I can give their too familiar name of Life Units. So as time went shapelessly by manufacture after manufacture was abandoned, skill after skill allowed to disappear from the Earth. Uniformity became more and more complete—a uniformity of plastic and concrete. Much the same thing happened with the cultivation of the land. At first it was easy enough, for numbers had been greatly reduced. But as the population crept up and up and every cranny was cultivated—completing the extermination of wild life which had already been carried so far —the dull, slow pressure of food shortage increased relentlessly. One response was to grow only foods which were the most economical source of nourishment; cattle, pigs and sheep were allowed to die out; a few goats are all you have been allowed to keep. The other response was enforced sterilization. Crown-bearers, I need not carry my history farther, for now it joins with your own experience, you know how it has gone and are pledged to bring it to an end. One curious exception there is which I myself can hardly understand. Why is it that the Unites have insisted upon flight, have devoted all their last skill to it, and used it with a thoroughness unknown before? Before the famines, Men had perfected flying without machines, but it was rare and little used. The early Unites perfected it. Partly there must have been a practical reason: flight saved road and railway space for agriculture, and also the metal of vehicles and ships. But I believe it means something more than that and something more hopeful. Just as man's need for emotional expression and for adventure has gone into the Tower, so something of his pride, his tradition of mastery finds expression in flight. It has gone astray, it has become a kind of degradation even as the Tower is a degradation, but it represents the spirit upon which we shall work.

' "Crown-bearers our revolution will succeed! We will restore to Man his ancient freedom for service, the dignity which lies in freedom to look up and to look down. Equality shall fall, but we shall again all be equals as Men confronted with the mystery of life. Here before you stand your symbols of light and of darkness, of flesh with spirit. When you have crowned the infant your King, he will be your possession, the embodiment of your common life."

'As he finished, Rachel, with the infant on her arm, came to stand beside him in the car, and from the shadows behind the African began to beat his drum.

'Sire, I left the Tower, and passed into the concrete waste outside where the dust was slithering in the night wind and the sound of the drumming spilled only faintly over the lofty walls. I was tired, perhaps even a little weary of these people and their struggles. It would be so

long, I thought as I lingered there between the tenements, so very long before they could climb back to the
height I had known. And they would have to take evil
with them. Yet I loved them.'

Finding him silent God addressed him, saying: 'I thank
you my trusted messenger; already while you are gone
these creatures of the Earth have returned to my consciousness; already I have gathered more of their gifts,
though not yet great ones, into the hollow of my hand.
Shall I have more and greater?'

'I believe, dear Lord, that you will. The Crown-bearers
assumed power with little violence. When I left Earth the
infant had been proclaimed King; the ancient crown was
held above him while he was anointed from the cup and
everyone there, even the most dazed and hardened of
them, knelt down with some feeling of holiness, with
some true emotion.' The Messenger continued, a note of
earthly irony still lingering in his voice: 'There is yet better cause for hope, my Lord; a greater certainty that you
will not be disappointed. I thought it would be well to
leave the planet at the exact point where I first alighted
upon it, and so, returning to the rock, I had an impulse
once more to see the Cave, to experience its present silence
and emptiness. When I passed the curtain I encountered
a smell familiar everywhere except in that place. Inside
on the Cave floor lay three Red Unites, sleeping noisily.
On the wall above the rock shelf they had stuck an old
plastic bill: "All Unites are born Equal and shall die
Equal. Unites the Human Race". So, Sire, the new Men
will find their opposition waiting for them. They will suc-

ceed, perhaps gloriously, in their revolution against equality and then equality will be again preached by the generous of heart. Your being will be nourished, never fear, with the struggles of these creatures again to be called Men. Once more your vision will be filled with the exquisite projections of their joy and suffering. They will never fail you while they inhabit the Earth.' He paused. 'I have one more request to make.' In response to the divine interrogation the messenger of God spoke once more. 'When I am refreshed and strengthened by steeping in your consciousness, grant, dear Lord, that I may return to Earth. The story there will be a long one, and I feel a great desire to follow it.'

Even above Life Unit 1457 the skies were lightened by the divine assent.

The Fossil Fish
and the Swimming Fish

CUTTING THROUGH sandstone, the waters of a river had exposed a fossil fish, an elegant creature with every scale glistening as though it were made of polished jet.

Several large salmon who had recently come up the river began to mock their distant kinsman. With their shapely fins and immensely powerful, muscular tails they swirled up and down past the ledge where he lay, rolling over on their sides as they boasted of their prowess as swimmers and of the long migrations which had carried them half round the world.

'That is really nothing to boast of,' said the fossil fish. 'I have never troubled to move, and yet, as you can see, I am here just the same.'

The salmon dropped to the river bottom, arguing and gaping among themselves.